LATINOS IN THE STRUGGLE FOR EQUAL EDUCATION

James D. Cockcroft

LATINOS
IN THE
STRUGGLE
FOR EQUAL
EDUCATION

The Hispanic Experience in the Americas

Franklin Watts
A Division of Grolier Publishing
New York—London—Hong Kong—Sydney
Danbury, Connecticut

For Eric—"in the trenches"

Frontispiece: Puerto Rican school children at the entrance to an East Harlem, New York, grammar school at lunchtime (1947).

Photographs copyright ©: UPI/Bettmann: pp. 2, 41, 47, 63, 67, 80, 81, 120; North Wind Picture Archives: pp. 15, 18; FSA/Library of Congress/Jay Mallin: p. 23; The Bettmann Archive: p. 57; The City College of New York City/CUNY: p. 99; School Improvement Services: p. 104; Board of Education, New York City: p. 105; Montana State Capitol, Office of Public Instruction: p. 135.

Library of Congress Cataloging-in-Publication Data

Cockcroft, James D.
Latinos in the struggle for equal education / James D. Cockcroft.
p. cm. — (The Hispanic experience in the Americas)
Includes bibliographical references and index.
Summary: Describes the struggle of Hispanic Americans to get an equal education, with an emphasis on New York City and the Southwest.
ISBN 0-531-11226-8
1. Hispanic American students—Education—Juvenile literature. 2. Educational equalization—United States—Juvenile literature. [1. Hispanic Americans—Education. 2. Education, Bilingual.]
I. Title. II. Series.
LC2669.C63 1995
371.97'68'073—dc20

95-8934
CIP AC

CONTENTS

ACKNOWLEDGMENTS

I wish to thank the many so-called minority students and teachers with whom I have worked over the years for giving me insight into problems in the field of education. Special thanks go to fellow writer and best friend Hedda Garza, whose creative ideas have inspired so many, and also to Constance Pohl for her continued excellent editing of the books in this series. And to the librarians and staff at Glens Falls' Crandall Library and SUNY-Albany's library I say "thanks again."

INTRODUCTION

They pledge allegiance to "one nation indivisible". . . . The nation is hardly "indivisible" where education is concerned. It is at least two nations, quite methodically divided, with a fair amount of liberty for some, no liberty that justifies the word for many others, and justice...only for the kids whose parents can afford to purchase it.
> —Widely published educational expert
> Jonathan Kozol, 1991[1]

The history of Hispanic education has been one of struggle against insensitive government agencies and school boards, those organizations responsible for governing education systems.
> —Michael A. Olivas, 1983[2]

When I am with a group of fellow Latinos I'm conscious of our differences. Cubanos, Mexicanos, Puerto Riqueños, Colombianos, we are all different. Yet when I find myself among non-Latinos I realize how much alike we Latinos are.
> —Participant in a 1982–83 study on
> education[3]

Most Americans are aware of the history of discrimination against African Americans. Our schools honor Martin Luther King's birthday and "Black History Month."[4]

But very little is ever said about the discrimination and social problems affecting Hispanics, or *Latinos,* as many prefer to be called when not recognized by their national background ("Cuban," "Dominican," "Colombian," etc.).[5] Few know that Latinos fought and won school desegregation cases at the local level long before the Supreme Court's 1954 *Brown* decision. Even fewer realize that Latinos were not officially recognized as covered by *Brown* until 1973, or that today they are more segregated in the school system than blacks. For a long time, Hispanics were "the invisible minority"—books on education rarely even mentioned them! Then, when they became more visible, they were all too often viewed by the rest of society as "the other"—something strange, fearful, inferior.

Inequalities in education affect everyone. The phrase "cultural deprivation" is almost always used to refer to Latinos or blacks. But whites also suffer from being separated from other peoples, often "ghettoized" in suburban bedroom communities and deprived of a worldly multicultural education.

Educational equality is not merely an issue of new schools, smaller classrooms, computers, racial segregation, or even bilingual programs to assist those not fluent in English. Underlying all of the educational problems are serious economic divisions. As Labor Secretary Robert B. Reich pointed out in 1994, "A society divided between the haves and have-nots or the well-educated and the poorly educated cannot be a stable society over time . . . [it] spells a breakdown somewhere down the line."[6]

This book, like the first ones in this series,[7] covers the little-known struggles for social justice by the nation's largest emergent "minority"[8]—this time focusing on the Latinos' fight for equality in education.

1
uno

LEARNING
WITHOUT
SCHOOLS—OR
DESPITE THEM

"Educar un muchacho es perder un buen pastor" ("To educate a boy is to lose a good shepherd").
> —Common saying among "ricos" (rich Mexicans in the Southwest)[1]

There were three elementary schools. One for Anglos made of permanent construction with several acres of play ground, one for Mexican Americans, a dilapidated one room frame building to serve first, second, and third grades. . . . The other school was for colored children.
> —Eleuterio Escobar recalling early 1900s' school days in Texas[2]

In early 1910, in the Mexican section of the bustling west-central Texas town of San Angelo, excited parents and children often talked about the almost completed beautiful new school building. Within weeks their elation turned into disappointment. The local school board informed them that their children would attend classes in the old frame building being abandoned by white "Anglo" pupils instead of their previous shacks that passed for schools.

The new building had more than enough space for all of San Angelo's children. Angry Mexican parents decided to withhold the names of their 200 school-age children from census takers. Since state aid to education, then as today, was based on the number of students counted in the scholastic census, the Mexican parents hoped the school board would reconsider their discriminatory decision.

The board countered with an offer of "separate but equal facilities" and ordered the census retaken. The phrase "separate but equal" came from the U.S. Supreme Court's 1896 *Plessy v. Ferguson* decision that legitimized racial segregation in public places if the facilities offered nonwhites were equal.[3] Mexican parents knew that "separate" was never "equal" in Texas. Their children attended school in ramshackle huts. They were taught by teachers hired with few educational requirements. Their battered textbooks were ones discarded by the white-only schools.

In Texas, the *de jure* (by law) segregation of blacks was reinforced by the practice of *de facto* (in fact) segregation of Mexicans and other Latinos. Worse yet, in many communities Mexican children had no schools at all. Local school board authorities would not allow them to enroll in "Anglo" schools and did not bother to provide alternative facilities for them!

In the early 1900s, fewer than one out of five Mexican children attended any school. An Anglo farmer explained: "if they get educated a little, they don't make such good farm hands."[4] Half of the school children were routinely absent at cotton-picking time. Only gradually were schools established in Mexican *barrios* (neighborhoods). As late as 1944 nearly half the Mexican children in Texas still received no school education.

Usually Mexican parents lacked the economic and political power to successfully challenge the authorities. They had been excluded from voting booths and jury boxes for generations by a poll tax and by various citizenship and English literacy requirements. But the education of their children was an issue dear to their hearts.

San Angelo's Mexican families decided to fight back. About 300 parents gathered together and voted to reject the school board's "separate but equal" proposal. One father told the local newspaper: "Under the system which now prevails, the Mexican children are learning nothing. . . . We have the right to put our children in the white schools." The school board president, an immigrant from England, countered: "the proposition of intermingling the whites and Mexicans would be a terrific blow and . . . demoralize our entire school system."[5]

The parents decided that unless their children received the benefits of state education aid for which they paid taxes they would boycott the schools. That September, seven neatly dressed Mexican children tested the waters by attempting to enter the new school house. Guards blocked their entrance.

After that some of the parents tried sending their children to nearby religious schools, where discrimination and high costs discouraged them. Youngsters were assigned to separate "Mexican rooms." Despite all the difficulties, the school boycott held firm for four years. Finally the Mexican parents returned their children to the free but still segregated public schools in 1915.

But their action had not been in vain. It touched off open debate on the issue. A well-known San Antonio Anglo educator called the policy of counting Mexicans for the school census but refusing to educate them "short-sighted." He pointed out that families packed up and left areas where their children were not provided with decent schooling, taking their "little fund" with them. "Many a little town," he said, "had lost good, steady labor and quite a good cash trade in that they have failed to see the business advantage of a neat, up-to-date school for its Mexican ward."

A superintendent of a segregated school district in Texas disagreed: "it is up to the white population to keep the Mexican on his knees in an onion patch or in new ground. This does not mix very well with education."[6] Others declared that Mexican children were intellectually inferior and that it would be a waste to attempt to educate them.

Not all Anglos agreed with these racist theories. Well-educated people knew about the distinguished intellectual heritage of Latinos, dating far back to ancient, highly advanced Indian civilizations as well as to Spanish traditions infused with Greco-Roman, African, Jewish, Christian, and Muslim learning.[7]

In 1916 W. G. Knox, a concerned white Anglo principal of a public school who had taught in a *barrio* school for most of his career in San Antonio, informed a journalist from the national magazine *New Republic* that he could detect "no characteristic intellectual differences between Mexican and American children." In fact, he found the Mexican child "more eager to learn than the American child . . . his parents are very interested in his progress." He concluded that "many of my best students are of the darkest types."[8] He was a lone voice in the wilderness.

The educational dilemma of Mexican Americans and other Latinos has its roots in early American history. The first European settlers of today's United States were not the English people who landed at Plymouth Rock but Spanish explorers. After conquering Mexico in 1519, parties of adventurers crossed the Rio Grande into today's Southwest, attempting to impose their authority on the agricultural and nomadic Indian tribes living in the area.[9]

The Spaniards set up fortified Catholic missions for

SantaYnez Mission in California. The Spanish settlers of the Southwest set up missions with schools that imposed European customs on the native people.

protection against the very Indians they hoped to "civilize." Those missions were the nearest thing to a "school" most people in the Southwest would see for a very long time. The Spanish rulers quickly decreed the abolition of indigenous languages and their replacement by Spanish. The mission "schools" quickly imposed European (later to be called *American*) customs and ways of life on the region's Native Americans.

Prior to the United States' winning Independence from Great Britain (1783) or Mexico's gaining independence from Spain (1821), education of any kind was largely reserved for the elite—almost always "white"—who dominated the economies and colonial administrations in the English Northeast and the Spanish Southwest (plus Florida). After independence, a racial pecking order was maintained, with Native Americans and a rapidly growing number of African slaves placed at the bottom of the social ladder. Generally speaking, the darker your skin color, the worse off you were.

After Mexico won its independence from Spain, it abolished slavery. But even under Mexican rule, today's Southwest remained enmeshed in a skin-color pecking order.

Scattered parish churches took over the tasks of the Catholic missions—but without the missionaries who had been expelled by Mexico with other Spaniards in the 1830s. New Mexico's first public education system was mandated in 1836. It taxed the lucrative Santa Fe trade route and the area's citizens to pay for a few public schools. The governor was killed in a taxpayers' revolt, however, and his forward-looking program was not enacted until many decades later.[10]

Meanwhile, English-speaking "Anglo" settlers in the Southwest established all-white private schools. After invading Texas to establish the slaveholding "Lone Star Republic" (1836) and then statehood (1845), they consolidated control over education as they expanded westward. Mexico was too busy fending off these attempts to seize more of its territory to pay much mind to education.

In 1846 the United States conquered California and invaded central Mexico, gaining possession of nearly half of Mexico's land and much of its wealth. The 1848 Treaty of Guadalupe Hidalgo, which formally ended the U.S.-Mexican War, guaranteed the cultural, educational, language, and property rights of those Mexicans choosing to remain in today's Southwest. The Anglos violated the treaty when they took over most of the properties and political power from the 100,000 Mexicans who stayed (60,000 of them in New Mexico). New Mexico's 1912 state constitution belatedly "guaranteed" the treaty's contents and called for training bilingual teachers for Spanish-speaking students.[11]

After the abolition of slavery and the end of the Civil War in 1865, a system of white racism continued to stamp Mexicans, like blacks, as "racially inferior." Although technically not segregated by the "black codes" and "Jim Crow" laws that followed the brief post-Civil War Reconstruction period, Mexicans were segregated by custom, language, voting laws, and residence—and viewed by most whites as little better than blacks.

Although denied access to the new schools gradually being opened up by Anglos in the Southwest, Mexicans generously offered the Anglo "newcomers" a unique education, teaching them their mining, ranching, and irrigation techniques, all instrumental in building up a prosperous Southwest. The Anglos rewarded their teachers by driving them off their lands and usurping their mine claims. In the Crystal City area of Texas (later to become an important center of the Chicano empowerment movement—see Chapter 4), Anglo "pioneers" "shot Mexicans for the fun of it."[12] As a later Chicano writer bitterly concluded:

> *Many millions of dollars in profits were realized from the toil and technology of those same Mexicans who were murdered, reviled, humiliated, and mercilessly exploited, who lived in shocking conditions in unsanitary shacks at the edges of the fields, along the tracks, in the depths of the mines . . . undergoing "schooling for a time in the meaning and methods of freedom."*[13]

Some Mexicans fought back, but they were outnumbered and outgunned by lawmen like the Texas Rangers, founded in 1835, and the Arizona Rangers, created in 1900. They were especially concerned about the education of their children, but rarely able to do much about it. Throughout the Southwest the so-called "Mexican wage" was far lower than the wages paid to other workers. Just to put food on the table, it was often necessary for Mexican

Scene on the Rio Grande. Mexican culture was a combination of Spanish and Native American influences. Mexicans were segregated in the Anglo-controlled Southwest.

children to work alongside their parents in the fields. Child labor and compulsory education laws were nonexistent. When Mexican laborers began establishing unions based on their mutual aid societies (*mutualistas*), they often tried to organize reading and writing lessons for the children, exhausted from long hours of work.

As social movements for workers' and women's rights gained momentum, reformers envisioned free public schools for everyone (although blacks remained segregated). Rapidly expanding northern industries needed disciplined, literate workers, and the first public schools provided a few years of schooling emphasizing the WASP (White Anglo-Saxon Protestant) values of discipline, obedience, and the work ethic. In those days the "work ethic" meant twelve- to fourteen-hour workdays.[14]

In Spanish-speaking areas of the nation, educators found it easiest to train future workers in their own language. Colorado legislated bilingualism in its schools. In Los Angeles a school ordinance stated that "all the rudiments of the English and Spanish languages should be taught."[15]

In the 1860s nearly half the students attending Los Angeles's few public schools were Spanish-surnamed. But as more and more white Americans flooded into the area, Mexicans were stripped of their wealth, relegated to the lowest-paying jobs, and excluded from the schools. English eventually became the only language of instruction. By 1880 only 6 percent of the students in Los Angeles' public schools were Mexican. Statewide, adult literacy rates among Mexicans had plummeted below 25 percent, compared with almost 85 percent for California's adult population as a whole. Since their petitions for admission to school, bilingual education, and equal treatment were denied, many Mexicans attempted to educate their children at home.[16]

The assault on use of the Spanish language—the so-called "No Spanish rule"—began even earlier in Texas.[17] By 1900 use of Spanish in the nation's schools was tolerated only in New Mexico, where Mexicans still vastly outnumbered Europeans.

As so often happened with other discriminated-against groups, the nation's Mexicans were negatively labeled by the dominant white culture—they were called "dirty Greasers." In Texas, a few Mexican children were sent to "Mexican" schools, but often there were none. El Paso, for example, had no "Mexican" high school until 1927. Texas school officials routinely justified school exclusion with statements like: "They [Mexicans] are an inferior race, that is all."[18]

In New Mexico and southern Colorado, light-skinned "ricos" called themselves "Hispanos" (of pure Spanish stock) to distinguish themselves from the poor majority of darker-skinned Mexican farmhands, shepherds, mineworkers, day laborers, and servants. Some well-off Mexicans "used their Anglo connections to send their children to parochial schools or apprenticeships in St. Louis."[19]

Intermarriages were not infrequent, especially in New Mexico where few Anglo women were available. In traditional Hispanic culture and law, females could own and inherit property. A wealthy Mexican wife was a "good catch" for an ambitious Anglo settler. While Anglos, ricos, and Anglo/"rico" couples made sure that their own children attended school, three-fourths of the Mexican children of their laborers never saw the inside of a classroom. Their elite *patrones* (bosses) were reluctant to lose their labor. To a degree, the same pattern evolved in Texas.

In California, as in Texas, Mexicans and other Latinos —Chileans, Peruvians, and Nicaraguans—were also denied equal education. Local school boards made the rules, and Latinos were seldom board members. In most places, it was necessary to be a registered voter in order to serve on such powerful educational bodies. English-only ballots, English literacy tests, and frequently changing residency requirements prevented most Latinos from ever running for office or winning an appointment. In Los Angeles, there were only three Mexican Americans ever seated on a school board in a period of 120 years—one in 1854, two in 1884, and then none until 1974.[20]

Even in predominantly Mexican southern Colorado and New Mexico, most school-board members, teachers, and administrators were Anglo. From 1850 to 1900 there was not one Hispanic state superintendent of public education in the entire Southwest.[21] Without people in positions of power to speak for them, Mexican children had little access to education. The few schools available to them were almost always located in their own segregated neighborhoods and therefore *de facto* segregated. Sometimes the children were officially segregated, categorized as Indians and therefore subject to laws requiring separate schools for Indians (Native Americans) and most Asian peoples, a policy that survived until 1947.

In the late nineteenth century, a period of massive industrialization, workers and their labor unions called for educational reform. Many of the new industrialists agreed. Thousands of immigrants arrived every week, most of them from non-Protestant Eastern and Southern Europe. They spoke many different languages—Italian, German, Polish, Yiddish. Not only did their new employers want them to learn the proper WASP values of hard work and obedience, but even more urgently they wanted them to drop their foreign cultures and languages entirely, trading them in for the English language and American way of life.

Free schools were introduced, usually segregating Latinos and blacks. Compulsory school attendance laws were also introduced (rarely enforced for Latinos, Asians, African Americans, or Native Americans).

"Americanization" through public school education was championed by powerful elites and a wide range of influential organizations, including several labor unions, the Daughters of the American Revolution, the YMCA, the Texas Rangers, and the Ku Klux Klan. Americanization completely dominated the new public school system until the 1960s, and—although continually challenged since then—it still prevails today. The goals of Americanization, although now stated in more careful terms, have also remained similar to those expressed by the dean of Stanford's College of Education, Elwood P. Cubberly, in 1909:

> [The immigrants are] illiterate, docile, lacking in
> self-reliance and initiative, and not possessing the
> Angloteutonic conceptions of law, order, and govern-
> ment. . . . Our task is to break up these [immigrant]
> groups or settlements, to assimilate and amalgamate
> these people as a part of our American race, and to
> implant in their children, so far as can be done, the
> Anglo-Saxon conception of righteousness, law and
> order, and our popular government. [22]

As new waves of immigrants from Eastern and Southern Europe poured into the country—more than twenty million between 1880 and 1924—most of them settled in the industrial cities of the East and Midwest. The public school system expanded rapidly in those areas. But it grew more slowly in the agricultural and mining regions where most Mexicans lived and worked. Chances for any Latino to attend school, even a segregated one, improved only slightly.

During those years, nearly an eighth of Mexico's population also emigrated to the United States, but many came to do seasonal labor—a million in 1926, for example. The children of seasonal workers, called "migrant laborers," were almost always deprived of schooling. Excluded from the occasional new child labor laws won by the trade-union movement, they followed the crops from place to place with their families.

In the East, especially in New York City, Puerto Ricans began to arrive in larger numbers. Most of them were required by law to attend the usually inferior schools in their own neighborhoods (see Chapter 3). [23]

Those Mexican children permitted to attend schools in

*Children of migrant workers, like the boy shown
here, often labored in the fields with their families
and were usually deprived of schooling.*

California, Texas, and the Southwest were forced to study
in English only, even if they had arrived the previous week.
Their textbooks told them little about their heritage, except
for an occasional lie or half-truth. Anglo heroes who had
fought against the Mexicans and captured the Southwest
were glorified for bringing "freedom and democracy."
Children who could not read the words sometimes looked

at the pictures and saw a stereotyped drawing of a Mexican peasant sleeping against a cactus plant, a huge sombrero protecting his face from the sun—the implied message being "Mexicans are lazy and dumb." Almost a century later, in the early 1990s, a recently published grade-school textbook in New York State sported this very same image on its cover![24]

The new emphasis on "American" culture in the schools hurt the self-image of many foreign-born children. One prominent educator later recalled: "We soon got the idea that Italian meant something inferior. . . . [in the schools'] process of Americanization, we were becoming Americans by learning to be ashamed of our parents."[25]

Other educational reforms, often well intended, also reinforced racism. The creation of separate classrooms for each grade, for example, which was meant to replace the overcrowded "one-room school house" for children of all ages, usually led to discriminatory "tracking." Children were assigned to specific classrooms according to the educators' perceptions of their likely future careers as blue-collar workers or white-collar professionals. Since almost all of the teachers were middle-class whites, they were not usually objective. Furthermore, since many of the children spoke little or no English, it was almost impossible to judge their learning potential.

Some educators from immigrant families objected to making the schools "an annex to the mill and factory" and a means of "choking off the ambitions of immigrant and lower-class communities." Riots broke out in 1917 against the plan, mostly in New York's Jewish neighborhoods, but the policy remained firmly in place.[26]

Undeterred, the advocates of the new public education system maintained their goals of molding every young person into an "American" destined for a certain kind of work. Famous philosopher of education John Dewey spoke of "education for all" in order to "Americanize" the heterogeneous population.[27] In a 1909 play, *The Melting Pot*,

Israel Zangwill dramatized the "Americanization" idea in a scene at Ellis Island:

> *Here you stand in your fifty groups, with your fifty languages. . . . these are the fires of God you've come to . . . into the Crucible with you all: God is making America.*[28]

In a 1917 patriotic appeal, former president Theodore Roosevelt celebrated "the melting pot," saying "it must turn them out in one American mold . . . the mold shaped 140 years ago by the men who under Washington founded this as a free nation."[29]

Only the nation's blacks, dark-skinned Latinos, and Indians were not expected to jump into the melting pot and assimilate, since the white power structure viewed them as "unmeltable," unacceptable. Famed African-American civil rights leader W.E.B. DuBois challenged the "Americanization" approach—but in vain. Several Indian, Latino, and other educators also expressed dismay at the mono-cultural and exclusive system being established.

Not only the schools but the popular culture of the day, like the widely read dime novels, championed Anglo-Saxon values and denigrated other cultures, especially non-white ones. The famous Horatio Alger series told stories of young boys from the slums "making it" through hard work, honesty, and thrift.

The reality was starkly different. Condemned by an anti-immigrant press, suffering from a school system that banned their languages and cultures and "tracked" them into low-wage, grinding jobs, only a trickle of immigrants and their children "made it." Many more died of tuberculosis and other diseases of poverty.

It became even more difficult for Latinos to improve their lot after 1910. As Mexico erupted in revolution against the ruthless dictatorship of General Porfirio Díaz and as the United States prepared to enter World War I to fight against Germany, a "Brown Scare" swept the nation, peaking in 1917. Especially targeted were those most likely to protest discrimination—anti-Díaz activists and Mexican trade unionists.[30] They were wildly accused of being "German spies" and "alien troublemakers." The 1917 Espionage Act and 1918 Sedition Act legalized deportations of non-citizens as "undesirable aliens." Mexicans and other Latinos, Jews, Italians, Slavs, and others were snatched up in the dragnet "Palmer Raids" of 1919–1920, when some 10,000 people, mostly union organizers, were arrested on orders from the Justice Department's A. Mitchell Palmer.

During that period, another educational "reform," intelligence theory, gained ascendance—with disastrous consequences for Latinos and many other immigrants for generations to come. "IQ" (intelligence quotient) and similar tests, including psychological tests, were introduced, becoming "the norm" by the 1920s. Under the guise of science, the new standardized tests were to "measure" and "determine" people's "intelligence" and "appropriateness" for different types of work.

Latinos and other immigrant children took the tests under several obvious handicaps. Reading speed and comprehension were vital components of achieving a high score. Naturally anyone with poor skills in English performed slowly and poorly on the tests. Often the questions themselves were "culturally biased," meaning that they contained little material familiar to children from Latino and immigrant homes. Economic and health conditions also had a negative impact on test scores. Because employers and society treated them as less than fully "American" or "equal," many Mexican parents earning "the Mexican wage" had to make immense sacrifices to provide even a semi-healthy, partially fed home. Children from poor families often came to school hungry and ill. Disease and malnutrition affected Latino homes far more than Anglo ones.[31] Famed Mexican American educator Dr. George I. Sánchez pointed out as early as 1932 that "intelligence tests are in part measures of environmental effects."[32] Since his pioneering studies, scientists have come to recognize that "intelligence" comes in many forms and that no single written test can possibly come close to "measuring" it.

The ridiculousness of the testing programs was clearly evidenced in 1913, when a psychologist applied IQ tests to new immigrants at Ellis Island, almost all of them speaking little or no English. Concerned about Southern and Eastern European immigrants outnumbering Northwestern European ones, he found roughly 80 percent of the Italians, Hungarians, Russians, and Jews to be "feeble-minded—and therefore deportable."[33] Worse yet, the testing programs became the norm nationwide, forming a so-called "scientific" basis for determining the educational futures of all children.

Based on IQ test scores, children were placed in classes for "gifted," "normal," or "slow" learners. Every schoolchild was well aware of his or her status as the member of a "smart" or "dumb" class. Those in "slow" classes often felt hopeless and defeated. Expectation of school achievement or lack of it became a self-fulfilling prophecy. Teachers of "intelligent" children tried their best. Those assigned to classes of "low" scorers tended to believe there was no point in struggling to teach "low IQ" children. The less the children learned, the worse they did on subsequent achievement tests. Latinos routinely fell behind in grade level and often were "pushed out" or "dropped out" rather than face further humiliation.

Sometimes, as one mother complained in the 1960s, "They pass the kids just to get rid of them. . . . [They] finish school and they still don't know how to read or write."[34] Not until the 1970s did occasional federal district courts find IQ tests racially and culturally biased, but standardized testing has increased in use right up to the present (see Chapter 8).[35]

Accompanying the rise of standardized testing was a

vigorous "eugenics movement" that led to dozens of states' passing sterilization laws for some of the "mentally retarded" and "criminal elements," also using test scores as a basis for such categories. By the 1920s, researchers, politicians, and educators were calling for a "biological housecleaning." Germans studied U.S. eugenics "science," later to apply their "superior race" theories to the extermination of six million Jews—the Holocaust. Press articles called Latinos a "eugenic menace." One popular pseudoscientific writer concluded that Mexicans were "inferior" and "born communist."[36] In 1980, eugenic sterilization laws were still on the books in twenty-six states.[37]

If schoolchildren from Latino families did not "measure up," then they were deemed "un-American" and "inferior." In the words of historian Gilbert G. Gonzalez: "Through the [school] program of Americanization, the Mexican child was taught that his family, community, and culture were obstacles to schooling success."[38]

To make matters worse, an unusually large portion of Latinos who persevered through more than three grades of schooling were told to repeat grades because of low test scores or "language difficulties," often one and the same thing. They also were disciplined or suspended from school more often than youth from other groups. Throughout the twentieth century, federal reports on Latino children in the schools documented their frequent physical punishment by teachers. Newly arriving teenage immigrants with high-school backgrounds were often placed in sixth or seventh grade. Suffering from "hazing" by the other students, neglect or physical abuse by the teachers, and a future without hope, many Latinos left school. A complaint commonly heard from them up to the present was: "I didn't drop out, I was pushed out." Today's prominent Chicano artist-playwright Harry Gamboa recalls his having "a dunce cap put on with a little lapel pin that said *Spanish*."[39]

Naturally, this racist atmosphere undermined the chances for Latino children to gain an equal education. One leading authority concluded in 1928 that "Probably the principal factor governing retardation of the Mexican child is his mental ability as measured by the group test." Another leading educator asserted that Mexicans were responsible for "bringing sickness and diseases of contagious sort and of causing poverty and lawlessness." The California *Guide for Teaching Non-English Speaking Children* recommended drills like a teacher's washing a child's hands and face and combing his hair and then presenting him before the class with the words "Look at José. He is clean."[40]

Lawmakers impressed with these racial and ethnic "findings" based the 1924 Immigration Act on them. They established a discriminatory quota system that assured a numerical majority of white people from Northwestern Europe. The one significant exception to the new restrictive law was Mexico, because low-paid Mexican farmworkers were needed to maintain the nation's commercialized agriculture boom.[41]

There can be little doubt that the "Americanization" phase of public education discriminated against other cultures and races in a way that reinforced the racial-ethnic pecking order of the job market. Of course, not just Latinos but almost all the nation's immigrants initially faced name-calling, negative stereotyping, and "tracking" in the schools. But a number of factors have made the struggle for educational equity and equal job opportunity especially difficult for Latinos.

First and foremost, the nonwhite skin color of most Latinos has made them vulnerable to racial discrimination based on color alone. No matter how hard they try, most Latinos cannot completely blend in and "Americanize" as most white Europeans (or white Latinos) can.

Second, unlike Europeans, most Latinos have come from countries in Latin America that have been militarily or economically controlled by the United States. This has meant that their cultures have not been awarded much respect. The result has been European-centered school textbooks that usually omit the noteworthy contributions of Latinos to the building of America.

Third, the Roman Catholic Church never assisted Latino Catholics as it did Irish or Italian immigrants. Hardly any priests were available in the Southwest in the 1800s and early 1900s. The Catholic Church was in no position to defy the U.S. "Protestant" takeover of Mexico's former northern territories. Realizing its comparative weakness, the Catholic Church decided to cooperate with the Anglos. It urged Mexicans not to resist the attacks they suffered, to await their "rewards in Heaven," and above all to "Americanize." Its few parochial schools jumped on the Americanization bandwagon.

Fourth, Latinos then and now have had family roots in nearby countries to which they can frequently return. This has added to their ability to maintain their own cultures in the face of the daily exclusion or discrimination they have faced in the "Americanization" and nativist campaigns.

On the other hand, most European immigrants have had little chance to return home more than once in a great while. They have known that the United States was their permanent home and so have emphasized adopting "American" ways at the expense of their own cultures.[42]

Fifth, unlike Latinos already here or just arriving, early European immigrants had another advantage in addition to white skin pigmentation. In the large cities where they settled they could attend free English classes at the many "settlement houses" being created by social reformers or offered at night by the public schools. Even so, only 13 percent of immigrant children in New York City's schools in 1908 went on to high school. As noted by one education historian, it is a "false legend" that the public school "took poor immigrant children and taught them so well that eventually they became prosperous Americans."[43] Many, in fact, dropped out of school but found jobs in the expanding economy.

Latinos were denied access to many of those better-paying unskilled and semiskilled jobs open to white immigrant school dropouts—in the garment, construction, and later steel and automobile industries. Although not as bad off as African Americans who suffered extreme racism, Latinos faced frequent employment discrimination. This in turn led to many being forced to live in miserable urban slums or rural shacks. Housing segregation became the basis for underfunded and understaffed local "Mexican schools" (because of low tax bases for school funding).

Even Latinos who could afford to live in neighborhoods with better schools were unable to purchase homes or rent apartments. Real estate companies routinely steered Latino and black customers to segregated housing developments. A 1933 Federal Housing Administration (FHA) report used as a guideline for insurance companies and real-estate appraisers indicated that the two groups with the most harmful impact on property values were blacks and Mexicans, reinforcing the prejudice and fears of white homeowners.

Middle-class Mexican women and other Latinas suffered from the double discrimination of sexism against all women and racism against Latinos. Even "upper-class" white college women in those earlier times were pushed out of the professions and onto a "home economics" track.

Of course, few Mexican women ever made it to college, but the "home economics" track assigned to elite women was meant for them too. Noting that Mexican girls would likely grow up to become waitresses or "house servants," a future teacher wrote in her 1938 University of Southern California master's thesis: "They should be taught something about cleaning, table-setting, and serving." The author of *Americanization through Homemaking,* an elementary school teacher's manual, openly admitted some of the real reasons for a home economics curriculum:

The man with a home and family is more dependable and less revolutionary in his tendencies. . . . the influence of the home extends to labor problems and to many other problems in the social regime. The home-

maker creates the atmosphere, whether it be one of
harmony and cooperation or of dissatisfaction and
revolt.

The author's choice of words reflected employers' fears of the frequent resistance to unfair treatment displayed by working people, including supposedly "docile" Mexicans.

There was truth in their fears, of course. Many educated Latinos in the United States have related in one way or another to the social movements of resistance to injustice. They were and are proud bearers of the Latin American "intellectual activist" tradition—people who use their education not just to understand the world but to change it for the better.

The anti-Mexican and anti-labor union violence of the World War I decade introduced a period of so-called "normalcy"—the 1920s. "Normalcy" meant that many of the "intellectual activists" had been silenced or deported, and others were too frightened to fight back. It also meant a new era of economic prosperity for a nation victorious at war.

For many Mexicans, whether at school, at work, or at home, the racist violence seemed never to let up. Nonetheless, despite all the obstacles, Latino parents continued to struggle to place their children in school. By 1930 they succeeded in enrolling nearly half the Latino school-age children in Texas and California. Anglos continued to try to keep them in separate schools for Mexicans—"the shack."

Americanization classes taught that the United States was a land of justice and equality, guaranteed by the Constitution and many laws. Those from the small emerging Mexican middle class decided to try a different tactic. They would test the validity of the lessons they had learned at school and go to the courts.

2 *dos*

GOING

TO THE

JUDGE

*The [San Jacinto Elementary School] board
had no right to separate these children two
miles away from the other children and put
them all in one room with only one teacher for
five grades and to share a playground fenced
with barbed wire.*

—LULAC protest letter, 1945[1]

They were Mexican Americans, some with parents and grandparents still living across the border in Baja California. In Lemon Grove, California, they had built a thriving community by working in the fruit orchards, a local mining quarry, and a railroad packing house. But they were always viewed as "the Other." So far as the white world knew, Lemon Grove was, as a local newspaper described it in 1926, "one of the prettiest spots in the San Diego suburban district. . . . the hills surrounding the town are covered with fine lemon and orange groves that are producing hundreds of thousands of dollars."[2]

On January 5, 1931, the principal of the newly constructed Lemon Grove Grammar School stood at the door and turned away 75 of the 169 children about to enter. They were children of the town's workers who, until that day, had never been separated at school except for special English classes. Now the principal told them they must attend a dismal-looking two-room structure they nicknamed *La Caballeriza* (the barnyard or horse stable). "No way!" said the children.

Newspaper headlines blared: "75 Mexican students go on strike! Parents Sue!" The children's parents obtained legal aid from the local Mexican consulate and took the school board to court. They wanted to set a precedent that would eliminate segregation throughout California. The children chose one of their smartest classmates, fluent in English, to represent them.

The children and parents knew that they risked losing everything they had because of the deportations of Mexicans taking place at the time. The nation was in the midst of the 1930s' Great Depression, when fourteen million persons of all races, a third of the workforce, could not find jobs. Entire families were on the streets in "soup lines," waiting for free food. Schoolchildren—500 of them in Chicago—were marching on local boards of education to demand school lunch programs. In Orange County, just north of Lemon Grove, the Santa Ana Board of Education deprived Mexican children of school lunches by limiting their schooling to the morning hours so that they could work the rest of the day "until the walnut season is over."[3]

Because of joblessness, a kind of mass fear gripped the nation. People were looking for scapegoats. Following the lead of the press and President Hoover, many falsely blamed more than two million of their fellow citizens, people of Mexican ancestry, for taking scarce jobs in decent paying parts of the economy. An official, highly publicized deportation drive aimed to rid the country of what one reporter called "Mexican mestizos, or half breeds . . . bringing countless numbers of American citizens into the world with the reckless prodigality of rabbits."

During the Lemon Grove children's school boycott, Mexican families gathered in downtown Los Angeles's "Placita Park" to visit and talk matters over. Suddenly, immigration authorities and police charged into the plaza from all sides and rounded up 400 people for deportation. They arrested anyone resisting, including some Chinese. The Spanish-language newspapers protested, but few listened. Raids on workplaces and *barrios* continued. Mexicans were hauled from public buses, their families broken up, their properties seized. Local train stations were packed with deportees.

"I'll never forget," one woman later recalled, "[how] they put all the people in boxcars instead of inside the trains."[4]

In California from 75,000 to 100,000 men, women, and children were shipped off to Mexico. Nationwide, of the more than half a million deportees, from 60 to 75 percent were U.S.-born children. In other words, American citizens were being kicked out of America for no other reason than their ancestry. For some children, educational equality was not a matter of being admitted to a decent school. It was a question of being let back into your own country.

The Lemon Grove school board was not worried about

the Mexican parents' court challenge. A board backer stated: "If this fails, we will slip a bill through the state legislature so we can segregate these greasers."[5]

As the school boycott continued, *barrio* families filled the courtroom and excitedly whispered translations to one another. The district attorney, serving as lawyer for the Lemon Grove school board, told the judge that the Mexicans had been separated because they were "older than the other children in corresponding grades."

The audience gasped.

This "was not segregation," the lawyer continued, but rather an attempt at "Americanization . . . wherein backward and deficient children could be given better instruction . . . [especially in] knowledge of English."

More gasps, cries of "Sinverguenza!" (Shame!)

Judge Claude Chambers, a former president of the San Diego Merchants' Association, leaned forward. Frowning, he asked the district attorney what the school did with other children who were behind in grade level.

"They are kept in a lower grade," the lawyer replied.

"You don't segregate them?" asked the judge. "Why not do the same with the other children? Wouldn't the association of American and Mexican children be favorable to the learning of English for these [Mexican] children?"

Now a hushed silence of expectation enveloped the courtroom.

Finally, Judge Chambers issued his ruling: the school's segregation policy infringed state laws, and the children must be reinstated immediately. "I believe," the judge intoned, "this separation denies the Mexican children the presence of the American children, which is so necessary to learn the English language."

The parents and friends of the seventy-five children wildly applauded the decision. They had no way of knowing that their courageous struggle represented the nation's first successful school integration suit—twenty-three years before the Supreme Court's *Brown v. Board of Education* decision of 1954 outlawing racial segregation in public schools and forty-two years before *Brown* was recognized as applicable to Latinos.

★ ★ ★

For a long time Latinos had been seeking not only admission to public schools but also the repeal of laws prohibiting instruction in any language other than English. These laws, existing in fifteen states in the early 1920s, left Spanish-speaking and many other immigrant children without a fair chance to learn. In 1923 the Supreme Court banned the English-only law in a case brought by German Americans (*Meyer v. Nebraska*). "The protection of the Constitution extends to all," the Court declared, "to those who speak other languages as well as to those born with English on the tongue."[6] Even though courts in several locales repealed English-only laws later in the 1920s, the "No Spanish rule" still prevailed in most schools.

Parents organized school boycotts on this and other issues. In 1928 in Dimmit County, Texas, Mexican families boycotted the school because of the insensitive way it treated their children. In Charlotte Independent School District, south of San Antonio, a parent won a decision by the state superintendent against segregating his daughter. In 1930, families tried to block the construction of a "Mexican school" in the border town of Del Rio, Texas. Facing defeat, they turned to a new civil rights organization for help, the League of United Latin American Citizens (LULAC).

LULAC contributed to some of the nation's earliest court victories against segregation, usually responding after community people mobilized. Rooted in south Texas, it established chapters throughout the Southwest. LULAC limited its membership to male citizens of Latin American descent. Membership was drawn largely from the less than 10 percent of the nation's adult Mexican Americans who had achieved some success as skilled workers, small businessmen, or professionals. These men sought to distinguish themselves from the "unskilled" Mexican immigrant workers who were so often deported as non-citizens.

By excluding immigrants, LULAC lost out on the contributions of many talented Mexicans. The immigrants joined more working-class-oriented organizations, like Texas's pecan sheller unions and California's cannery worker unions, whose strikes LULAC opposed. LULAC's exclusion of women also cost it valuable contributions from a wide range of female activists. Not until 1934 did LULAC create "ladies councils" for their participation.

Like the NAACP (National Association for the Advancement of Colored People, founded in 1910), LULAC advocated a litigation approach to civil rights. Realizing that the courts might not rule in their favor since Latinos were routinely excluded from juries, LULAC decided to fight the Texas poll tax and discrimination in jury selection. Finally, in 1954 the Supreme Court banned discrimination in jury selection.[7]

LULAC's middle-class members wished to assimilate into the so-called "melting pot." The organization made English its official language and referred to "Mexican Americans" as "the first white race to inhabit this vast empire of ours." In 1936 it won a suit against the Social Security Administration that reversed a decision to require Mexicans to designate themselves as "Mexican" instead of "white" or "other white."

One of LULAC's first cases against school segregation occurred when its founders responded to the pleas of Del Rio's parents in 1930 (*Del Rio Independent School District v. Salvatierra*). Del Rio's Mexican parents complained that their children were being illegally segregated. The court initially agreed, ruling that Mexicans were "white" or "other white." But an appellate court accepted the school district's argument that the segregation was based on the need to teach students English, even though the school superintendent had acknowledged that "the best way to learn a language is to be associated with the people who speak that language."[8] On the other hand, the appellate court acknowledged that school segregation based on race was unconstitutional—an early precedent, like Lemon Grove, for the 1954 *Brown* desegregation decision.

In 1934 a LULAC committee in San Antonio's west side *barrio,* where one-fourth of school students were Anglos, scheduled a rally to demand improved school conditions for *all* students. The committee head was a hard-working third-grade dropout named Eleuterio Escobar who was fervently committed to educational equity. More than 10,000 people showed up for the rally, but school authorities ignored their demands. Disappointed LULAC leaders at the state level, who fancied themselves a cut above working-class types like Escobar, expelled Escobar without consulting the *barrio.*

People responded instantly. They formed San Antonio's La Liga Pro-Defensa Escolar—the School Improvement League, a coalition of seventy organizations representing 75,000—with Escobar elected as its spokesperson. The League conducted a twelve-year battle to improve the area's overcrowded, run-down schools. It succeeded in placing more Latino teachers, administrators, and school-board members.

Meanwhile, Latino parents in other parts of the country organized to win equality in education. Many also became active in the labor union movement. Workers' strikes and popular protests pressured President Franklin D. Roosevelt to introduce reforms known as the "New Deal." By the late 1930s, the huge union movement won federal laws outlawing child labor and mandating the eight-hour work day, a minimum wage, unemployment insurance, workmen's compensation benefits, and social security. One of organized labor's most prominent Latino leaders was Guatemalan-born seamstress and college graduate Luisa Moreno. She and Mexico-born Josefina Fierro de Bright, a sociologist, helped found the 6,000-member Spanish-Speaking Peoples Congress ("El Congreso," 1938–1942).

Among El Congreso's chief sponsors were LULAC "intellectual activists" like famed folklorist Arthur L. Campa and educator George I. Sánchez.[9] El Congreso called for many reforms, including the introduction of unprejudiced, multicultural textbooks and the creation of "culture schools" to educate the public about Latinos—ideas being reintroduced today. At the college level, El Congreso advocated special departments to explore Latino and Latin American history and culture—a policy implemented thirty-five years later as a result of the Chicano empowerment movement.

The 1930s Depression ended with stepped-up armaments production for World War II against the totalitarian racist regimes of Nazi Germany and Japan. The Nazis under Hitler had started the onslaught against the Jews, and the Japanese were slaughtering the people of China. Naturally, Latinos and African Americans hoped an antiracist war to defend "democracy" meant a fairer school system for them. They also sought an equal chance at the new defense industry jobs opening up.

The government responded in 1941 by creating the FEPC (Fair Employment Practices Committee) to look into discrimination by private companies with government contracts. Carlos E. Castañeda, a Mexican-American history professor from the University of Texas and one of the few Latinos teaching in the nation's colleges back then, became FEPC regional director in Texas.[10]

Starting in 1942, some fourteen million Americans, including half a million Latinos, went off to fight the war. The United States worked out a treaty with Mexico, known as the Bracero Program (1942–1964), to import contract labor to make up for the sudden shortage in railroad and agricultural workers. These *braceros* were treated like slaves, their children shut out of the educational system. Yet millions of them helped save democracy by keeping goods moving for the war effort.[11]

To help combat the Nazi threat in the Western Hemisphere, the government created the Office of Inter-

Mexican farm laborers in a trailer truck leave U.S. Immigration Border Patrol headquarters for the farms of New Mexico's Pecos Valley as part of the Bracero Program.

American Affairs (OIA). It introduced a "Good Neighbor" curriculum into the nation's schools. Prominent Mexican-American educators like Sánchez and schoolteachers like Connie Garza Brockette became important OIA officials. They and others influenced the Texas state education department to issue calls for educational equality, including an end to school segregation. As one educator, H. T. Manuel, stated: "Neighborliness, like charity, should begin at home."[12]

The Latinos, especially professors Sánchez, Castañeda, and Campa, sparked a nationwide effort to introduce inter-American and Latin American history and culture into the public school curriculum. Sánchez advocated adapting the school to the child instead of the child to the school—an idea now widely accepted among educators. An educational psychologist, Sánchez explained how nonadaptive schools harmed a Latino child:

> *He cannot speak to the teacher and is unable to understand what goes on about him in the classroom. He finally submits to rote learning, parroting words and processes in self-defense. . . . Of course he learns English and the school subjects imperfectly!*[13]

Under pressure from Sánchez and others, some schools began to overlook the "No Spanish rule." This concession and the Latin America curriculum, however, were dropped right after World War II.

At the very time these pioneering educational efforts were taking place, white racist violence increased. In 1943, some white sailors went on a rampage in Los Angeles and other *barrios,* beating up on Latinos, Filipinos, and blacks while police and Navy officers stood aside. The press blamed the brawling on Mexican "zoot suiters." Racial tensions exploded throughout southern California. Later, Mexican war veterans returning from action in World War II organized the Latin American Organization (LAO) to demand justice in not just this matter but also in education.

In wealthy Orange County, the Santa Ana Board of Education had long refused Latino parents' requests to have their children transferred out of condemned wood-frame buildings to an "American" school. By the mid-1940s, a quarter of Orange County's enrolled school children were Latino. Some of the parents gave false addresses to smuggle their kids into the better schools. The Board discovered what they had done and expelled their children. The parents, working with the LAO vets, sought legal aid.

Parents in other Orange County school districts began protesting too. Just fifteen miles from Santa Ana, in the small farming community of Westminster, Mexico-born Gonzalo Méndez and his Puerto Rican wife Felicitas demanded school integration. Like so many of their neighbors, the Méndezes had been raised picking oranges and other crops. Recently they had begun to prosper, leasing a sixty-acre vegetable farm from a Japanese family that had been interned in a detention camp after Japan's bombing of Pearl Harbor. When Westminster Elementary School, which Gonzalo Méndez had attended *before* it had become segregated, refused to enroll their children, he and Felicitas raised a fuss. They demanded access to the school for everyone, including the thirty farmhands they employed.

The local authorities tried to make a deal—the Méndez children could attend but not the others. The Méndezes said they would not tolerate integration for "a mere handful of fortunate ones."[14] They obtained a lawyer and linked their protest to the ones going on in Santa Ana and other communities. Together they filed a victorious pathbreaking "class action suit" that became known as *Méndez v. Westminster School District, 1946, 1947.*

The Méndezes put up most of the money for the case, and Felicitas Méndez initiated a grassroots parents' group that filled the courtroom in 1946. The Méndezes told their lawyers to insist that the *Plessy* doctrine of "separate but equal" must be overturned. To the surprise of some, the federal judge of the Ninth District Court completely agreed with the Méndezes, affirming that "separate but equal" had no place. He based his ruling on both the Treaty of Guadalupe Hidalgo and the U.S. Constitution's Fourteenth

Amendment "equal protection" clause. "Schools," he said, "must be open to all children . . . regardless of lineage."[15]

Even more significantly, an appellate court unanimously upheld the judge's ruling in 1947. Lawyers around the nation quickly realized that the *Méndez* decision contradicted the 1896 *Plessy* doctrine of "separate but equal." It laid the groundwork for the famed 1954 *Brown* decision that smashed *Plessy* nationally. It also reaffirmed that English could be learned more easily in mixed than in segregated schools, assuming there was special language instruction in the early grades by competent teachers.[16]

Toward the end of 1947, California's legislature, responding to *Méndez,* struck down educational codes that had legally mandated segregation of Indian and Asian children. *De jure* school segregation was finally dead in California. During all the legal battles, attorneys from the National Lawyers Guild and the ACLU helped out. They were aided by LULAC, the NAACP, the American Jewish Congress, and the Japanese-American Citizens League. With unity came strength.

Meanwhile, the veterans of Santa Ana's LAO formed a LULAC chapter to extend the desegregation struggle nationwide. Latino parents in Chicago, Detroit, Kansas City, and elsewhere demanded equal education. In a typical action of the times, they launched an eight-month school boycott in a community outside Houston, Texas. The boycott forced San Jacinto officials to abandon an old barbed-wire-enclosed "Mexican school" depicted in the opening quotation of this chapter and to integrate a new modern school building.

Civil rights victories in other arenas helped the school desegregation fight too. Latino vets in Texas launched the American G.I. Forum in 1947 to protest a funeral home's denial of burial for a Mexican American killed in the Pacific. Mexican American soldiers had won more Medals of Honor than any other racial or ethnic group in World War II—the war against racism. They were not about to be pushed around by racists at home. "If we admit the damning theory of racial superiority," Professor Castañeda pointed out, "we are no better than the Nazis."[17]

In Washington government officials were sensitive to charges like these. In the "Cold War" against the Soviet Union, initiated in 1946–1947, the United States championed "freedom" and "democracy" against "communist tyranny." Anti-colonialist, pro-democracy leaders of Africa, Asia, and Latin America, diplomatically supported by the Soviet Union at the newly created United Nations headquartered in New York City, saw no Communist racism that could possibly match the South Africa–type segregation of schools and other institutions in the United States.

Pressured both at home and abroad, President Truman ordered the Armed Forces to desegregate in 1948. He also established a Fair Employment Board in civil service, although it lacked enforcement powers.[18]

In 1948 Minerva Delgado and twenty other parents in Texas won a fiercely contested antisegregation case, *Delgado v. Bastrop Independent School District. Delgado* forbade placing Mexicans in separate schools and represented one more nail in the coffin about to bury *Plessy.*[19]

Despite these local victories, school segregation continued, leading to the creation of civil rights groups more aggressive than LULAC. Two were the Community Service Organization (CSO) and the Asociación Nacional México-Americana (ANMA—National Mexico-American Association). The CSO advocated nonviolent street protests. One of its leading activists was Cesar Chavez, future farmworkers' union spokesperson (see Chapter 4). ANMA (1949–1955), founded by Latino miners in northern New Mexico, built unity among workers of different races and national backgrounds. It was about the only organization in the nation that had the courage to speak out against the hysterical anticommunist witch-hunt ("McCarthyism") that fed off the Cold War.[20]

In 1951 ANMA helped George I. Sánchez found the

broad-based American Council of Spanish-Speaking People. ANMA officer Virginia Ruiz declared that for Latinos to win any civil rights struggle they would need "to have the closest unity with our strongest ally, the Negro people."[21] Council members allied with the NAACP to win a court case against segregation in the elementary schools of El Centro, California. All across the country African Americans had begun organizing lunch counter "sit-ins" and other actions to end segregation. Black and Latino veterans of World War II and the Korean War injected a fighting spirit into what was already being called the "Civil Rights Movement."

The watershed event occurred in 1954: the *Brown* school desegregation decision. According to evidence in government briefs filed for civil rights cases leading up to and including *Brown,* a key factor in the 1954 Supreme Court decision was "the Cold War imperative"—the need to eliminate apartheid at home in order to justify charging the Soviet Union with human rights violations.[22]

In *Brown* the Supreme Court declared:

> *To separate . . . [children] from others of similar age and qualifications solely because of their race generates a feeling of inferiority. . . . We conclude that in the field of public education the [Plessy] doctrine of "separate but equal" has no place. Separate educational facilities are inherently unequal.*[23]

There followed a period of virulent white racism against blacks and Latinos to resist school integration. In the South, several terrorist organizations besides the Ku Klux Klan sprang up. At the same time, the Korean War ended and the country plunged into an economic recession. People looked for scapegoats.

So did the federal government. In 1954–55, its "Operation Wetback" deported some 1.5 million "Mexican" workers, many of them U.S. citizens. One Chicana later

In 1954 these young men were arrested and deported as part of "Operation Wetback."

told an interviewer: "I remember, as a child, just getting under the table, just scared to death, because they'd come in with those great big guns and they'd point them at my father."[24] Mexico-born Ernesto Galarza, author of *Merchants of Labor*, the pioneering work exposing agribusiness's rise to power on the bent backs of Mexican *braceros*, said "Operation Wetback" was being used to intimidate Latinos seeking equal rights. But his and ANMA's protests fell on deaf ears.

In 1959, after fierce legislative battles, LULAC won state funding in Texas for its "Little School of 400" program initiated with LULAC funds two years earlier. It taught 400 words of basic English to preschoolers. The highly successful program became a model for the national Head Start Program so widely acclaimed today.

From the mid-1940s until the mid-1960s, despite periodic recessions, the nation experienced unprecedented economic prosperity. The Cold War kept defense industry booming, and new technologies changed the face of the world. Youth attended schools in larger percentages than ever before. Latinos and blacks, however, remained heavily segregated and negatively "tracked," despite the *Brown* decision. The U.S. Office of Education sponsored "life adjustment education" aimed at the 60 percent of secondary school students who fit neither the college-bound track nor the "desirable skilled occupations" track. Latinos filled the "life adjustment education" classes—ones with names like "improvement of personal appearance" and "dancing and party stunts."[25]

In order to justify continued segregation after *Brown*, school boards invoked the doctrines of "freedom of choice" and "states' rights." In 1968 the Supreme Court ruled that local "freedom of choice" schemes could no longer serve as a "good faith" effort to end school segregation as required by its 1955 "*Brown II*" ruling. The decision led to the controversial busing of children out of their home neighborhoods in order to desegregate schools. Initially this did not help Latinos since they were not covered by *Brown* (partly attributable to LULAC's successes at defining Latinos as "white" or "other white").

Not until the 1970s did the courts mandate school desegregation for Latinos. In *Cisneros v. Corpus Christi Independent School District, 1970, 1971*, a U.S. district court and an appellate court ruled that Mexican Americans are an "identifiable ethnic minority with a pattern of discrimination" and therefore covered by *Brown*.[26] But other courts in Texas and Florida ruled otherwise!

A Supreme Court decision in Denver (*Keyes v. School District No. 1 Denver, Colorado, 1973*) finally resolved the issue. Denver blacks pointed out that school boards were falsely claiming successful desegregation by lumping Mexican Americans into the "whites" category. In this way, a school with mostly blacks and Latinos was considered "integrated." The Court ruled this was wrong—Latinos must be covered by *Brown*.

Despite the *Keyes* decision and the growing availability of busing schemes, local and state school officials continued to raise the issues of residential concentration patterns and "local school autonomy" to avoid compliance. Consequently, Latinos were left with the old problem of "Mexican schools"—or *escuelas de burros* ("dumb schools"), as one Mexican "push-out" (dropout) remembered their being called in Los Angeles' *barrios*.[27]

From 1968 to 1986, the percentage of Latinos attending predominantly nonwhite schools rose from 54.8 percent to 71.5 percent, while that of blacks dropped from 76.6 to 63.3 percent.[28] Discouragingly, despite all of the court battles, Latinos are more segregated in the nation's schools than African Americans.

3 *tres*

FIGHTING

CITY

HALL

I would like to have good teachers because some teachers like to hit the children so the children don't come to school because of that. Some school don't give good lunch and some of the windows are broken. The chairs aren't good. . . . Some teachers don't teach us in every subjects. So the children don't learn a lot. So the teachers leave them back.

—Sixth-grade composition by a
Puerto Rican youth in East
Harlem, New York City, 1965[1]

It was the early 1960s, but Manhattan's Lower East Side neighborhood looked pretty much as it had at the turn of the century. Many of the same rat-infested tenements remained standing, as they do today. Electrical wires hung overhead, telephone poles had replaced gaslights; cars had replaced horses and buggies; and corner grocery stores and supermarkets had replaced the peddlers hawking their wares in the teeming streets. The one major difference was that many of the immigrant Jews and Italians had moved out, and Latinos, mainly from Puerto Rico, had taken their place.

On East 4th Street, between Avenues C and D, just a short hop away from the East River, Spanish-speaking boys and girls crowded each day into the old public school that was once filled with Yiddish- and Italian-speaking children. Dutifully obeying the dress codes of the school administration, the youngsters entered their classrooms in what some of their parents called "bankers' uniforms"—starched white shirts, pressed pants, and neckties for the boys; dark skirts and white blouses for the girls. Their mothers, many of them working in New York City's garment factories, often stayed up late into the night, bleaching, washing, and ironing their children's school outfits, unable to afford duplicates and triplicates of each expensive costume.

Just ten blocks uptown in the white middle-class apartment complex of Stuyvesant Town, the children attended the neighborhood elementary school in easy-care Chinos, jeans, and polo shirts.

Like other Latino parents around the nation, Puerto Rican mothers and fathers were passionately concerned about the education of their children. Despite their long work hours, so many of the mothers regularly attended Parent-Teacher Association (PTA) meetings that school officials shifted them to the auditorium.

At one such gathering, a question period followed the report of the PTA president. Usually the women didn't say much, embarrassed by their own limited English and never encouraged to speak in Spanish. This time though, one mother, new to the neighborhood and more certain of her English, rose to her feet and asked about the dress code.

"How come our children have to wear fancy pressed pants and skirts and white shirts when the kids in Stuyvesant Town can come to school in play clothes? Most of us work all day and it's really hard to do this. I spend at least an hour every school night just washing and ironing dirty white shirts. And do you know how much these kinds of clothes cost if you want to buy more changes?"

The room came to life as women raised their hands and one after the other complained about the rules. Most had not even known about the dress code differences between "uptown" and "downtown" schools. One PTA official snapped at a mother who spoke in Spanish, "Please speak in English!"

Immediately, a mother in the back of the room jumped to her feet. "That's another thing!" she shouted. "The teachers hit our children whenever they speak Spanish. We can't help it if you speak only one language and we speak two—that's your problem, not ours. Why don't you start respecting us for a change?"

Applause spread through the auditorium. When things calmed down, everyone in the room concluded it was time to make some serious changes in how the Latino children were being treated. Faced with this sudden confrontation, school officials quickly changed the dress codes and promised to look into the parents' other concerns.[2]

★ ★ ★

Like the Mexicans, people from the Caribbean islands of Puerto Rico, Cuba, and the Dominican Republic have been in the United States for a long time. In the nineteenth century, they settled here in small numbers, some of them fleeing Spain's political repression and continuing the struggle against Spanish colonialism from a safer distance in New York City, Miami and a few other cities.

Schooling was practically nonexistent at first, but people learned in other ways. At the cigar factories where many worked, *lectores* (readers) read newspapers and poems to the men and women bent over piles of tobacco leaves twelve and fourteen hours a day. They listened avidly to the news reports on the fight against Spain, frequently interrupting the *lector* to argue and ask questions. The *lector* practice was first introduced in Cuba by followers of renowned poet-essayist José Martí, the so-called "Apostle" of Cuban Independence, killed in battle in 1895.

In those early times, Latinos from Florida to New York City were more interested than most immigrant groups in political events. Tobacco and factory workers, as well as intellectual activists like Puerto Ricans Eugenio María de Hostos and poetess Lola Rodríguez de Tío, closely followed the progress of the fight for freedom from Spain. Moreover, as Puerto Rican cigar worker Bernardo Vega later recalled in his memoirs, the exiles' early political clubs, cigar labor unions, newspapers, and mutual aid networks made adjustment easier for later arrivals.[3]

Just as Cuba's armed revolutionaries, many of them runaway slaves, were on the verge of winning independence from Spain in 1898, the U.S. battleship *Maine* mysteriously exploded and sank in a Havana harbor.[4] Ignoring a last-minute offer by Spain to cede Cuba to the United States, President McKinley used the *Maine* incident to justify a declaration of war. Thousands of Latinos attended anti-war rallies in New York and other cities, organized by the half-million strong Anti-imperialist League.

After the swiftly concluded war, the United States made Puerto Rico, the Philippines, and Guam its colonies.[5] A U.S.-appointed governor ruled Puerto Rico for almost half a century. New schools were constructed and the "Americanization" program was transferred to Spanish-speaking Puerto Rico. Under the 1900 Foraker Act, all classes were taught in English and children pledged allegiance to the American flag. In 1928, when the Puerto

Rican legislature asked U.S. President Calvin Coolidge for "the freedom that you enjoy . . . and have promised us," Coolidge bluntly stated that Puerto Ricans were "ignorant, poverty-stricken and diseased, not knowing what constituted a free and democratic government."[6]

The obvious racism of the President's remarks increased the resistance of the children, their parents, and teachers to the "No Spanish rule" in the schools—what they called linguistic colonialism. They finally won the right to teach and learn in their own language in 1949.

In 1917, a month before U.S. entry into World War I, the U.S. Congress passed the Jones Act, making Puerto Ricans U.S. citizens, without the right to vote in national elections but eligible for the draft. Some 18,000 young Puerto Ricans were inducted into the U.S. military.

During the early twentieth century, a handful of U.S. sugar companies took over Puerto Rico's best lands. *Jíbaros* (displaced peasants) labored long hours for little pay on lands they had once owned. More schools were built, but as future Governor (1948–1964) Luis Muñoz Marín said in the late 1920s, Puerto Rico became "a land of beggars and millionaires . . . [with] many more schools for . . . hungry children."[7]

As Puerto Rico's sugar industry mechanized, even low-wage jobs became harder to find. Because Puerto Ricans were U.S. citizens, it was easier for employers in the United States to recruit them than immigrants from Europe. Thousands of Puerto Ricans headed for the farm fields and plantations of the eastern seaboard, Arizona, and Hawaii. Tiny Puerto Rican settlements sprang up in faraway places like San Francisco and Chicago. But sooner or later most Puerto Ricans headed for New York City.

The city's garment industry owners needed their labor, especially after passage of the restrictive 1924 Immigration Act. They "contracted out" to operators in San Juan on a "homework" basis and also brought in tens of thousands of skilled Puerto Rican needle trades workers. Most were young, able to endure the cramped second-class "steam-boat shuttle" from San Juan to New York. Once they arrived they were welcomed by the established Puerto Rican community, which helped them to find jobs and housing. Most of the women worked as sewing machine operators in stifling "sweatshops." Those with children often took "piecework" home, looking after their babies as they bent over high piles of unassembled collars and sleeves. Women also took in lodgers, cared for neighbors' children, and worked as domestics. Men worked long hours for numerous light industries, construction firms, restaurants, and hotels.

Most of these newcomers dreamed of returning to the sunny shores of home—Puerto Rico. Puerto Rican parents in the United States—the "mainland"—were willing to toil long hours in the hope that their children would be well educated and never have to work long hours at grinding jobs. But they learned quickly that most of the public school administrators and teachers had a low opinion of their children's ability to learn, even as they often do today. Former Chicago school teacher Felix Padilla, a prominent sociologist, has offered one explanation:

> *The schools in el barrio are administered by whites; whites teach in the classroom and design the curriculum—not to meet the needs of Puerto Ricans but to Americanize them. . . . [children] are scorned for speaking Spanish in school. . . . made to feel ashamed of their Puerto Rican cultural traditions.*[8]

White racism came as a great shock to most Latinos, especially Puerto Ricans. The majority of Puerto Ricans were mulatto. Mixed marriages, encouraged by the Catholic Church, were common back home.[9]

Some Caribbean intellectuals on the mainland found it easier to identify with the nearby African-American community in Harlem. As early as 1911, Arturo A. Schomburg, a black Puerto Rican researcher who had participated in

*Arturo A. Schomburg, a black Puerto Rican researcher and
once a member of Jose Marti's Cuban Revolutionary Party,
compiled extensive information on black history, which he used
to found the New York Public Library's Schomburg Collection
on African-American history.*

José Martí's Cuban Revolutionary Party, helped create
Central Harlem's now world-famous Schomburg Collection
on African-American history.[10]

By 1926 Puerto Ricans numbered nearly 100,000 in
New York. East Harlem, a former garbage dump that had

become "a dumping ground for the poor,"[11] gradually became known as "*El Barrio*" or "Spanish Harlem." It was their main "colonia." They filled sprawling, overcrowded tenement buildings that had been built prior to the 1901 housing codes mandating central heating and bathrooms. Other Puerto Rican colonias developed in the south Bronx and in Brooklyn's waterfront area.

The "newcomer" Puerto Ricans were resented by some of East Harlem's Jewish and Italian residents. A race riot broke out during a July heat wave in 1926. The *New York Times* claimed that the disturbances were caused by rivalries between white merchants and peddlers, on the one hand, and Puerto Rican peddlers and owners of *bodegas* ("mom and pop" grocery stores), on the other. Out of these unpleasant events, new coalitions developed in East Harlem. Puerto Rican organizations like the Hermandad Puertorriqueña (Puerto Rican Brotherhood of America) worked with Jewish organizations to improve intergroup relations. The Brotherhood went on to spark a citywide unity drive among all Latinos, leading to the creation of La Liga Puertorriqueña e Hispana to protect Latin American culture and defend it against racist attacks.

Because "home" was so close, Puerto Ricans preserved their own language and culture, resisting "Americanization" more than most immigrant groups. Developing their own music also helped them to survive in the cold and often hostile North. When families found eviction notices under their doors because they fell behind in rent payments during the 1930s' Great Depression, musicians played at "rent parties" to help raise the needed dollars.

When racism hurt their children, the Puerto Rican community rushed to defend them. In 1936, massive IQ testing of schoolchildren became a major issue for New York's Puerto Ricans. Looking for scapegoats for the Great Depression, newspaper articles were cheering on the mass deportation of Mexicans and calling for similar actions against Puerto Ricans, branded as "criminals" and "paupers."[12] When the press publicized a New York State Chamber of Commerce report that claimed to prove that Puerto Rican schoolchildren were "mentally deficient" and "intellectually immature," activist intellectuals and parents in "El Barrio" fought back. The report based its findings on the results of intelligence tests in English administered to 240 Puerto Rican children.

Josefina Silva de Cintrón, editor of *Revista de Artes y Letras* (Arts and Letters Magazine), immediately published a stinging editorial criticizing "the educational harassment of Spanish-speaking youngsters" in the schools.[13] Silva de Cintrón and many parents realized that the Chamber's "findings" would reinforce the unfair practice of placing Puerto Rican children two or three grades back and calling them "dumb," instead of helping them to learn in their own language while they studied English. Placement in lower grades with much younger children made Puerto Rican youth feel foolish, bored, and rebellious. An elementary school teacher from Puerto Rico and early feminist, Silva de Cintrón joined with thousands of New York's Puerto Ricans to launch a campaign for bilingual education.

Puerto Rican trade unionists, newspapers, hometown clubs, youth groups, and La Liga Puertorriqueña e Hispana pitched in to help. The parents organized Madres y Padres Pro Niños Hispanos. They offered their services as teachers' aides in bilingual classrooms. La Liga recommended the formation of a Spanish-speaking teachers' committee and submitted a list of several suitable candidates—but its ideas were ignored by the white power structure.

An occasional New York politician, sensitive to Puerto Ricans' concerns, joined the struggle. One was Vito Marcantonio, himself raised in a Harlem tenement. East Harlem's congressman from 1934 to 1936 and 1938 to 1950, Marcantonio earned the nickname "Puerto Rico's congressman." Whenever there was a major problem, Puerto Ricans could count on his support. He denounced the

Chamber of Commerce's "most slanderous attack . . . on Puerto Rican children," saying that the *Psychological Clinic*'s publication of the report proved "there is such a thing as racketeering even in the field of psychology."[14] Marcantonio initiated an investigation refuting the Chamber's report and entered it into the *Congressional Record.*

It was not difficult to find more than enough facts to prove the absurdity of the Chamber report. A Columbia University Teachers College team in 1925 had tested 1,000 children in Puerto Rico on the Pintner Non-Language Mental Ability Test, *administered in Spanish,* and found that they exceeded American norms for grades three to five. The Columbia report concluded, "there is no reservation in our minds concerning the capacity of the Puerto Rican to . . . make profitable use of the type of intellectual education that more progressive school systems of the modern world are developing." Years later, in 1953, a study of New York's preschool Puerto Rican children would conclude that they were "fully on a par in intelligence with other children, and superior in linguistic ability."[15]

Racist attitudes, unfortunately, are not based on facts. Stuck with their preconceived notions, very few "intelligent" educators noticed the many signs of intellectual vitality in "El Barrio." Puerto Ricans regularly attended lectures and plays presented in Spanish. The city's first major Spanish-language daily newspaper, *La Prensa,* and other publications enjoyed wide readership. While many Americans remained ignorant of "foreign" affairs, Puerto Ricans were strongly aware of events in their homeland and other nearby countries.

In 1937, for example, when U.S. troops opened fire in Ponce, Puerto Rico on a peaceful parade honoring independence martyrs and asking for the release of imprisoned pro-independence fighters, twenty men, women, and children were killed and more than a hundred wounded.[16] Ten thousand Puerto Ricans in New York City immediately joined a protest march against "the Ponce massacre" and "Yankee imperialism."

One of the political prisoners was "activist intellectual" Ponce lawyer Pedro Albizu Campos, the Harvard graduate leader of the Puerto Rican Nationalist Party's movement for independence in the 1930s and 1940s. Many mainlanders identified with Albizu Campos, calling him "El Maestro" (The Teacher). Congressman Marcantonio became co-counsel for Albizu Campos.

During World War II more than a thousand Puerto Ricans were hired as postal workers, many of them serving as mail censors because of their bilingual fluency. Community educators pointed out that it was necessary to pass difficult civil service exams to obtain these jobs, clear evidence of how smart Puerto Ricans were despite the education system's abuses and the Chamber's scurrilous report.

Voting has always been considered evidence of intelligence. When Puerto Ricans found someone worth electing, they rushed to the polls, despite literacy tests in English imposed to prevent them from voting. Educated Puerto Ricans joined forces with educated Jews and other concerned citizens to help potential voters pass the required tests. Puerto Ricans helped elect Marcantonio to serve in Congress for years and also supported Fiorello La Guardia in his campaigns for the New York mayoralty post. La Guardia, part Italian and part Jewish, became an early champion of Puerto Ricans' rights as U.S. citizens. The Puerto Rican community voted in the thousands several times, helping to keep La Guardia in the mayor's office from 1934 to 1945, when he declined to run for a fourth term.[17]

Despite the support of a few politicians and other friendly whites, the perpetuation of anti–Puerto Rican racism, relegation to the worst-paying, most undesirable jobs, and their children's ongoing difficulties with the schools took its toll on morale. It seemed to many Puerto Ricans that they were locked permanently in the status of second-class "citizenship." Only African Americans were placed "below" them in the social pecking order. Accordingly, many fell into the trap of taking great pains to distinguish themselves from "*los negros*" ("the blacks").

Piri Thomas, the dark mulatto son of a Puerto Rican mother and a Cuban father, wrote a much acclaimed memoir in which he described the difficulties of negotiating the color barriers in the 1930s and 1940s. Piri remembered applying along with a white friend for a door-to-door salesman's job in 1945. The Irish American interviewer told Piri the sales territory was already filled up. Then his friend was called in and quickly hired.

Some time later, Piri told an African-American buddy the story. The black man said, "Hell, Piri . . . a Negro faces that all the time."

"I know that," Piri answered, "but I wasn't a Negro then. I was still a Puerto Rican."[18]

Despite the racism, or perhaps because of it, Puerto Ricans persisted in their fight for equal education. Many Puerto Rican intellectual activists understood fully the necessity of allying with African Americans. They founded the Council of Puerto Rican and Spanish Organizations of Greater New York in 1952. The Council held street rallies against "Jim Crow"-type school segregation responsible for the inferior teaching and rundown conditions at *barrio* and African-American schools.

Traditionally, for many decades, New York City's Board of Education turned down applications from people with even slight Spanish accents trying to become accredited teachers. When the Civil Rights Movement of the 1960s put pressure on to find more Puerto Rican teachers, this policy was only gradually changed. To their surprise, recruiters found fully credentialed teachers from Puerto Rico working in the city's factories.[19]

Prior to the 1960s, educators like Puerto Rican school teacher María E. Sánchez, who came to New York with her husband in 1953, were permitted to serve as "Substitute

El Barrio, or Spanish Harlem, in New York City

Auxiliary Teachers." The auxiliaries worked long days at low wages assisting the regular teachers, counseling students, and serving as liaisons between schools and the Puerto Rican community. Sánchez and her compatriots organized the Society of Puerto Rican Auxiliary Teachers, which fought for and won auxiliary licensure.[20]

Fifteen years later, María E. Sánchez played an important role in New York City's new bilingual education programs (*see* Chapter 4), but the road to victory often appeared impassable. The ideas were out there but always ignored. From the 1930s on, determined Puerto Rican educators had long been brainstorming some of the nation's first plans for bilingual and equal education for Latinos. The New York City Board of Education drew on their ideas in its well-funded 1958 report, *The Puerto Rican Study, 1953-1957.* It contained a detailed set of recommendations for bilingual-bicultural education, improved teacher training, more Puerto Rican teachers, fairly administered and culturally unbiased tests, and community involvement. Unfortunately, the report was shelved and Puerto Rican teachers continued to serve as powerless "auxiliaries."

During and after World War II, the Puerto Rican population in the United States swelled. By the end of the 1950s, nearly half of Puerto Rico's population lived on the mainland, most of them jamming into New York City's slums, their children packed into already overcrowded, inadequate schools. Few made the choice to leave their homeland happily. They came because economic conditions in Puerto Rico deteriorated, the pay was better in New York, and airplanes made the trip easier than in the old days.

In his insightful 1961 book *A Puerto Rican in New York and Other Sketches*, Jesús Colón (1901-1974), an activist worker-intellectual of African-Puerto Rican heritage, convincingly explained the reasons for Puerto Ricans' economic problems. When Luis Muñoz Marín became Puerto Rico's first elected governor in 1948 (after first renouncing his pro-independence stance), his administration completed a reform project known as "Operation Bootstrap" that shifted the island economy from its sugar base to industry. U.S. manufacturing plants moved to Puerto Rico to take advantage of its low wage structure and the absence of federal income taxes.

As the new industries installed the latest technologies, there were not enough jobs to go around. To deal with the unemployment problem, the Muñoz Marín government subsidized so-called thrift flights in dangerous nonpressurized airplanes to ship hundreds of thousands of people to the United States. Most of them worked as migratory farm workers and low-wage industrial and service employees. The island government also sought to control population growth by initiating a program that succeeded in sterilizing one-third of Puerto Rican women of reproductive age. As a means of making the island's colonial status less obvious, the government conducted a referendum in 1952 that created today's Commonwealth of Puerto Rico, "a free state in association with the United States." The ballot choices did not include independence, and Puerto Ricans still could not vote in U.S. national elections.[21]

As population pressures diminished, Puerto Rico's government, responding to popular demand, spent a third of its budget on education. A 1957 U.N. report noted that of all the countries in the world, Puerto Rico had the highest proportion of people (over a third of the island's residents) enrolled in some kind of formal education from kindergarten to college and adult education. School attendance increased to 85 percent of teenagers. This was further proof, if any be needed, that Puerto Rican parents were very committed to educating their children.[22] Equally committed Latino parents in New York City, as well as other places where Puerto Ricans had settled to find work (Boston, Bridgeport, Jersey City, Philadelphia, Cleveland, Chicago, and a few other cities), found that educational opportunities for their children had grown worse.

Many families traveled back and forth between Puerto Rico and the United States, switching jobs while their children changed schools (and languages). While some Puerto Ricans, including World War II veterans using the G.I. Bill, attended college and achieved better careers, most became locked into the secondary labor market reserved especially for them. By the 1980s, according to various reports of the U.S. Civil Rights Commission, Puerto Ricans were the most economically impoverished of all minority groups in the United States, second only to Native Americans. Ford Foundation researchers commented that the "devastating circular migration" back and forth between the island and the mainland had proved "disastrous for Puerto Rican families, employment, and income."[23]

The impact on schoolchildren was particularly destructive. As early as 1960 a writer of a major book on Puerto Ricans observed that elementary school textbooks used throughout the city bore "little relationship to the streets" of Latino barrios.[24]

In the late 1950s, Puerto Rican educator Antonia Pantoja joined with other professionals to create New York City's Puerto Rican Forum to seek out new business and career opportunities for Latinos. Pantoja, granddaughter of a tobacco worker, had taught school in rural Puerto Rico. In 1944 she had come to New York and worked as a factory welder and union organizer and then gone on to college, earning a master's degree at Columbia University's School of Social Work in 1954. She dedicated her life to improving race relations and life opportunities for Latinos. Realizing career promotion required college degrees, Pantoja and others launched Aspira (meaning "strive" in Spanish) in 1961 to promote higher education for Latinos.

In 1964, some Forum leaders and others founded the Puerto Rican Community Development Project. It mobilized campaigns against racial discrimination in schools, housing, and employment.

Puerto Rican activists like Aspira's Pantoja and Hilda Hidalgo (who later headed the Department of Community Development and Urban Studies at Rutgers University's Livingston College) fully understood the scope of the problems confronting Latinos in the nation's school system. By the early 1960s, census data showed that only 13 percent of Puerto Ricans on the mainland twenty-five years of age or

In 1958, Spanish-speaking children of New York City register at an East Harlem community center that provides social and educational activities.

older had completed high school. Worse yet, in New York City there were only 230 Puerto Ricans among 40,000 teachers (less than half of one percent).

These activist intellectuals pulled *The Puerto Rican Study* off the shelf, dusted off its covers, and demanded its implementation. An Aspira-sponsored national conference of Latinos in the 1960s reiterated the study's core ideas and publicized a report Aspira had commissioned on sixteen schools in seven cities, indicating that very little had changed. The conference issued fresh recommendations, but only a few were ever carried out.

The Ford Foundation agreed to fund Aspira's efforts to establish chapters in Newark, Philadelphia, Chicago, and San Juan. "Leadership clubs" formed, attracting 3,000 high school youth, but the Puerto Rican school dropout rate remained high, and Aspira knew that "leadership clubs" alone could not resolve the problem. Many schools stuck with the "No Spanish rule" and there were still too few Latino teachers. New York City's Board of Education continued to resist hiring teachers with Spanish accents or surnames. The school situation in Chicago was even worse.[25]

A Puerto Rican historian in the early 1970s wrote about the world he had grown up in back in the 1950s. "It was a world of unsympathetic and bigoted social workers and teachers," he recalled, "brutal policemen, broken families, small children bitten by rats and young men and women driven by their surroundings and hopelessness to crime and drug addiction."[26]

Most other Americans were unaware that those were the conditions for most Puerto Ricans. A 1965 report on Latinos by the National Education Association carried a revealing title: *The Invisible Minority*. With a long history of struggle for equal education behind them, Latinos were about to become very visible—by taking their struggle directly and explosively into city streets and school hallways from coast to coast.

4
cuatro

TAKING CONTROL

OF THE

CLASSROOMS

[The Chicano movement] was the turning point of my life because I became involved. . . . The "60s" were great years for us. We learned how to defend ourselves.
> —Jesusita de la Cruz, 1980[1]

Until we [Puerto Ricans] make this decision to fight and to do so beside our natural allies— black people with whom we share problems most directly in the cities; other Spanish-speaking Americans with whom we share a language and a tradition—we will remain a furtive presence wherever power resides.
> —Professor Frank Bonilla, 1968[2]

I keep fighting because I want my grandchildren to have what I and my children never had.
> —Retired Chicano sheet-metal worker
> Demetrio Rodríguez, 1994, in court
> controversy over equal school funding.[3]

In 1963 the life-size statue of Popeye in front of the City Hall of Crystal City in South Texas's Winter Garden area offended the Mexicans and Mexican Americans who were the majority of the city's 10,000 residents. The statue symbolized the prosperity of the 1920s when Anglo farmers had used cheap Mexican labor to make Crystal City "the spinach capital of the world." But it reminded many parents that the "city fathers" had initially denied the city's Mexican children any schooling and then limited their attendance to "Mexican schools." It wasn't until 1946 that a Mexican American was allowed to attend the city high school. After the *Brown* decision, the city's elementary schools admitted only those Latinos able to pass language proficiency exams.

Now they still had no influence on how things were done. But they were getting ready to correct that. This seemingly "peaceful migrant backwater" would be the first to eject Anglos from decades of ruling the school system.

Times were changing. In the area around Crystal City the California Packing Corporation (today's Del Monte) had bought up choice farm acreage, built a canning plant, and allowed the Teamsters to organize a union. The nation's economy was booming because of expanded defense production stimulated by the Cold War. Agriculture was mechanizing and the country was urbanizing at a rapid pace. Many Mexican farmworkers were settling in small cities like Crystal City and large ones like Los Angeles, helping to make Mexican Americans the nation's most urbanized people. Outside the cities, low-cost "prefabricated" housing projects appeared like magic, and many white workers moved to the suburbs. Consumer goods were abundant, and almost every home or apartment had a television set and a refrigerator or freezer.

In southern states like Texas, the old rural-based Jim Crow traditions were beginning to totter. African Americans, with several persuasive leaders in their ranks, including Martin Luther King and Malcolm X, had stepped forward to claim their rightful share of "the American dream." The young civil rights movement faced a stubborn resistance to school integration though.

Many of the nation's younger Mexican Americans, including those in Crystal City, were talking not only about the civil rights movement but also about the farmworkers' unionization drive headed by people like Cesar Chavez and Dolores Huerta—leaders of the National Farm Workers Association (later called the United Farm Workers, UFW). They were following the news about Reies López Tijerina and The Federal Alliance of Land Grants that had forcibly seized ancestral lands they claimed belonged to them under the Treaty of Guadalupe Hidalgo. And they were talking about electing some Mexican-American candidates in order to change the schools.

Crystal City residents, the Teamsters union, teenage students, and PASSO (the Political Organization of Spanish-speaking Organizations, an outgrowth of the Viva Kennedy Clubs of the 1960 presidential campaign) carried out a successful voter registration drive. Organizers helped farmworkers pay the $1.75 poll tax through an installment plan. Substantially outnumbering registered Anglo voters, they then voted out Anglo incumbents of the city council and elected five Mexican working-class candidates in 1963.

"Crystal City Revolt!" screamed headlines across the state. Incensed Anglos encouraged the Texas Rangers to harass "the greasers." They also quietly reconstructed their political machine by bringing in a few more prosperous Mexican Americans. A former high school student-body president, José Angel Gutiérrez, wrote an anonymous pamphlet denouncing what he called Mexican "Uncle Toms" (later to be known as "Tío Tacos") for siding with the Anglo power structure. Gutiérrez was kidnapped and threatened with death by local power figures and their henchmen.[4]

The newly elected Chicano city council lacked any real power. The city manager and Del Monte still held the upper hand. Then, in 1965, the refurbished Anglo political machine narrowly won the council elections by running "their Mexicans." They allowed two Mexican Americans to join the seven-man school board, and in the next few years the number of Chicano school teachers rose to 25 percent of the total.

Meanwhile, 250 miles to the south in the Lower Rio Grande Valley's Starr County, "the great melon strike of 1966" galvanized all of South Texas's attention. Farmworkers sympathetic to Chavez's UFW refused to harvest the cantaloupes for the area's major agribusiness. Texas Rangers stormed through Mexican migrant workers' shacks beating up strikers. College students and faculty members visited the farm fields and brought back word of the abuses, igniting indignation among Mexican Americans and leading to a statewide solidarity movement that developed too late to win the strike but fueled an expanding student movement.[5]

At that time, Chicanos were rising up angry everywhere. In Denver, Rodolfo "Corky" Gonzales, a poet, Presbyterian leader, and former boxer, was launching The Crusade for Justice. Emphasizing family unity, economic improvement of the *barrios*, and demonstrations in the streets, the Crusade established its own school and proclaimed: "We intend to nationalize every school in our community."[6] In California Chicano students and their parents were promoting community control of schools. Some 150 miles southeast of Crystal City, Gutiérrez was organizing a student youth movement at Texas A&I, a college in Kingsville.

In 1967, Gutiérrez's group expanded into a new statewide organization, the Mexican-American Youth Organization (MAYO). A year later the Ford Foundation gave MAYO a small grant for community development. Many LULAC leaders and politicians like U.S. congressman Henry B. González criticized Ford for funding MAYO's "student militants."

San Antonio lawyer Pete Tijerina went to New York to

try to raise money for a new civil rights organization more in tune with the times than LULAC. In conversations with officials at the Ford Foundation, he realized how "invisible" Latinos still were: "they did not know we existed. . . . [I]t was up to us to convince them of the police brutality, the segregation in schools, denial of fair trials."[7] He succeeded in convincing the foundation to provide $2.2 million in a five-year grant for the 1968 founding of MALDEF—the Mexican American Legal Defense and Education Fund, a major civil rights organization today. Ten percent of the Ford grant went to pay for law school scholarships for Chicano students.

Word of the "Crystal City Revolt" had spread to Ford and also to Washington. In 1967 President Lyndon Johnson agreed to hold a conference on Mexican American problems. It took the form of Cabinet hearings in El Paso, Texas. Several Chicano leaders were invited to participate, but not Cesar Chavez, Corky Gonzales, or Reies López Tijerina— a snub equivalent to keeping Martin Luther King, Jr., from attending a meeting on African Americans' civil rights. Other invited Latino leaders walked out to hold an alternative conference in El Paso's *barrios*. Calling their group La Raza Unida (United Race), they proclaimed: "the time of subjugation, exploitation, and abuse of human rights of La Raza in the United States is hereby ended forever."[8]

As a result of the new militant activism, more than fourteen million dollars of new federal "cool-out" monies poured into Crystal City for Head Start programs, better school facilities, pavement for *barrio* streets, and low-income housing. In 1969 the Texas state legislature removed statutes that had allowed schools to ban instruction in Spanish.

It looked as though the Chicano revolt had been subdued, but it soon became apparent that the changes at Crystal City's schools were more cosmetic than real. Quite a few "Mexican haters" remained among the faculty and administrators, sometimes telling Mexicans "you should feel privileged to sit next to whites." Chicano students fumed. They, their parents, and MAYO organized a strong campaign to reform the schools. When Crystal City school officials balked at granting even the mildest of their demands, such as the fair selection of cheerleaders, they stormed out of the classrooms and called a school boycott. MALDEF supported the boycotters and their demands: removal of racist teachers; more Latino staff; creation of bilingual and bicultural programs; end of censorship of the student newspaper; recognition of the Mexican national holiday September 16th; general equalization of educational conditions; a grievance procedure, and no punishment for strikers.

Immediately threatened with violence, three Crystal City students rushed off to Washington, D.C., and returned with two mediators from the Justice Department. When local officials still resisted change, the community launched a boycott of businesses firing workers who backed the student strike. The Teamsters, cozying up to the Nixon White House and planning an organizational drive against Chavez's UFW, did not help out. So the Chicanos started an alternative union and a campaign to decertify the Teamsters Union.

On January 4, 1970, the school board caved in to almost all the student demands—an unprecedented victory! That spring, veterans of the 1930s' school antisegregation struggles, such as María Hernández, joined the young militants of MAYO and others to found La Raza Unida Party, headed by Gutiérrez. Assisted by MALDEF, La Raza Unida candidates swept the city council and school board elections in Crystal City, as well as those in nearby towns. The party spread to other southwestern states and California, running candidates who drew thousands of votes.

The newly elected Crystal City school board introduced programs to encourage students to graduate from high school and go on to college. The high school opened its doors to adults—often the students' parents—so that they could complete studies for the high school diploma equivalency exams. When state officials blocked the school board's reforms and refused to provide teacher training, the board recruited instructors from Chicago State College and San Francisco State College. One teacher was indicted for conducting a history class in Spanish (the case was later dismissed). At that time, full-time college students were normally exempted from the military draft. Student activists in South Texas, as well as other parts of the nation, however, often were arbitrarily reclassified by local draft boards and shipped off to Vietnam, where America's longest war in history raged on.[9]

La Raza Unida established a community school in Crystal City as a training ground for Chicanos from other states, offering them classes about the roots of *"la raza"*— the race of Mexicans and Native Americans who had long resisted conquest. The example of Crystal City inspired Chicanos everywhere. Its rebellious spirit, like that of the striking melon pickers in Starr County, shattered once and for all the "stereotype of Juan Tortilla, a loyal servant happiest when he is stooped in the fields picking spinach for the Anglo."[10]

Two typical scenes from the mid-1960s helped explain why Latinos everywhere were beginning to demand more control over what went on in school classrooms. One was written up for the *National Education Association Journal* of May 1969 by former school teacher and then state senator Joe Bernal of Texas. The other was reported by a graduate student researching a typical New York City "mixed neighborhood" elementary school.

In the first scene, Ector, a popular six-foot Chicano varsity football player, leaned over to borrow a pencil from Juan.

"Traes un lapiz?" he asked.

Mrs. Jones, the teacher, snapped, "I've warned you about speaking Spanish in my class. Go see the vice principal right now, Ector."

Mr. Neill, the vice principal, gave Ector the familiar

fifteen-minute lecture on why it is "very American" to speak English, referring to the "No Spanish rule."

Ector thought to himself: "I know I'm as good an American as he is. My brother is in Vietnam and I'll probably be going too."

Mr. Neill gave Ector a choice: "three licks [with a whip] or your parents?"

Ector knew his father would miss work to come to school, and Ector's mother couldn't speak English.

"The three licks," he answered.[11]

In the second scene, a third-grade teacher, Miss Dwight, complained to her friends Edith and Mary in the teachers' room: "What really bothers me is all the talking in Spanish. And I'll flip if just one more child calls me 'teacha' today."

"Yeah," said Edith, "when they speak Spanish, they really prattle like monkeys. I'm sure they're not even trying to learn English."

"Wait," said Mary. "Remember that Spanish is natural to them. How would you like the pressure of learning a new language and new subjects all at the same time?"

"Mary," said Edith, "you're entirely too sympathetic. You live in a dream world. Do you really think for one minute that these kids will ever amount to anything? . . . They act like animals too. All you see in the newspapers are gang wars, dope addicts, and rapes."[12]

Other widespread teacher attitudes about Latinos detected by researchers included sentiments like the following: "*We* did it despite discrimination, why can't they?"; "The only way to teach them is to repeat things 25 times"; and "Many of the Mexican children just don't want to learn."[13] A California high-school dropout and gang member recalled in the 1980s how his teacher had "hated us to speak Spanish, so I spoke up. 'I was born a Mexican and I was blessed to speak two languages.' She replied, 'I'm sorry you were born a Mexican.'"[14] A Dallas high-school Latina remembered how "I told the counselor I wanted to go to college, but she said, 'Have you thought about beauty college?' Beauty college! That's all she thinks we're good for."[15]

The prestigious 1966 Coleman Report on *Equality of Educational Opportunity* cited additional school abuses of Latinos:

> *A vocational student hoping to become an electrician did the same wiring job for four consecutive years, over and over and over again.*
> *A [Puerto Rican] junior high school student was accused by his teacher of lying because he averted his eyes when speaking to her, a sign of respect on the island.*
> *A teenager told his principal he would have to drop out if he wasn't given protection from assaulting gangs whose turf lay between home and school. The principal referred him to a psychiatrist.*[16]

Numerous government reports documented racial biases, a Eurocentric (European-centered) curriculum excluding Latino peoples' true histories and cultures, "tracking," poor counseling, and inferior or segregated classrooms—all of which contributed to the high dropout, or "push-out," rates among Latinos. Most, like the Coleman Report, concluded that race and class barriers were even more important than language-cultural ones in contributing to Latino students' feelings of hopelessness and self-doubt.

A U.S. Commission on Civil Rights (CCR) report in the early 1970s noted that "significantly less is spent to educate Chicano children than their Anglo counterparts." Bilingual programs were reaching only one out of every forty Mexican-American students in the Southwest, remedial reading courses only 10.7 percent of them. The CCR report observed that school notices in the Southwest went out in English to four million parents whose mother tongue was Spanish, having "the effect of denying equality of educational opportunity to Spanish-surnamed pupils." The "No Spanish rule" still served as "a deterrent to Americanization" and resulted in the "discouragement" and "discipline" of its "offenders." Then, in a dramatic turnabout from the traditional Americanization approach, the CCR report concluded: "It is the responsibility of the school and the teacher to accept the child as he comes to school and to orient the program to his cultural and linguistic needs."[17]

This radical change in official attitudes would have been unthinkable in the absence of the powerful Civil Rights Movement. Not only Chicanos in the west but Puerto Ricans in the east intensified their struggles for equality. Dr. Kenneth B. Clark, a prominent black psychologist whose earlier legal brief on the damaging effects of school segregation had influenced the *Brown* ruling, had said: "I am not willing to sacrifice the kids while waiting for integration and while they attend criminally inferior schools."[18] Puerto Rican parents and youth felt the same way.

In 1964 they joined a boycott of New York City schools called by blacks to protest their failure to integrate. One observer called it "the first time in the [East Harlem] community's history, or the city's, that Puerto Ricans joined with Negroes in protest and pursuit of a common goal."[19] In the South Bronx the United Bronx Parents, mostly Puerto Ricans, formed an alliance with concerned blacks to improve the area's schools. Often blacks and Puerto Ricans were contesting over scarce resources, however, and tensions sometimes arose between the two groups.

Responding to the mass marches of the Civil Rights Movement, the U.S. Congress passed several pieces of civil rights legislation, including the 1965 Elementary and Secondary Education Act (ESEA) that provided for compensatory education for children affected by poverty. In 1968 a lengthy study of the nation's schools concluded that ESEA had been insufficient and even irrelevant. That same year the 1968 Bilingual Education Act was passed, becoming Title VII of the ESEA. Teacher-activist María E. Sánchez promptly obtained funding under Title VII to organize New York City's first bilingual kindergartens; she then created a bilingual education major for teacher trainees at Brooklyn College.

A House of Representatives special report noted that the country need "no longer be thought of . . . as a melting pot, which tends to homogenize all the various elements, but instead as a mosaic which gains it beauty and strength from variety and diversity."[20] Yet the melting pot was rapidly becoming a boiling cauldron, the mosaic a shattering mirror. As racial tensions ratcheted up another notch, several major cities exploded in destructive and costly rioting, filling the skies with billowing smoke and flames. Blaming white racism and poverty, the 1968 *Report of the National Advisory Commission on Civil Disorders* concluded that the country was "moving toward two societies, one black, one white—separate and unequal."[21]

In 1966 Chicago's Puerto Rican community rioted for two days in protest of a policeman's shooting of a young Puerto Rican man. Some Puerto Rican gang members rejected gang rivalries and founded the Young Lords to demand community control of police, better schools, and improved services. The push by gangs for social reform spread to other cities. In New York, the Sociedad Albizu Campos, a group of students and college dropouts, helped organize the Young Lords Party (YLP). The YLP called for "a true education of our Afro-Indio culture and Spanish language," as well as equal rights for women and independence for Puerto Rico. Appreciated by ghetto residents, Young Lords chapters set up day-care centers, breakfast-for-children kitchens, and "people's health clinics."

By the late 1960s, New York's Puerto Rican and African-American parents and children were leading a city-wide struggle to win "community control" of the schools. They wanted to wrest control of the classrooms out of the hands of what many viewed as racist teachers and administrators led by the United Federation of Teachers (UFT) and the Council of Supervisors and Administrators (CSA—principals and their staffs). By introducing multicultural

Ocean Hill-Brownsville school governing board
in front of Brooklyn J.H.S. 271

and federally mandated bilingual programs, they hoped to reclaim their place in history eroded through generations of "Americanization." Asian Americans quickly joined them. Also lending support were militantly antiracist white students and teachers, many of them Jewish. As in the Crystal City "La Raza" programs, a small number of college students and teachers linked up with New York's movement for better schools.

New York's "community control" movement was partly a response to the "disruptive child" clause of the UFT's proposed 1967 contract. The clause called for granting teachers the right to bar unruly students from their classrooms without a hearing or "due process." The Negro Teachers Association objected, but to no avail, and with-

*United Federation of Teachers pickets
in front of Brooklyn J.H.S. 271*

drew from the UFT. The First Citywide Conference of the Puerto Rican Community convened to add its voice to the protest.

It was a tense day when schools opened in September 1967. UFT teachers were absent in large numbers, unofficially striking until acceptance of the "disruptive child" clause. The situation quickly polarized into a near race war. In the midst of the controversy, the mayor's office issued a stinging report by a six-person committee that included Puerto Rican educator Antonia Pantoja and was chaired by Ford Foundation president McGeorge Bundy. The "Bundy Report," as it became known, called for calming things down by "decentralizing" the school system and granting more "community control," although not at the price of sacrificing the necessary influence of other important voices in public education such as the UFT and CSA. Because the report was critical of the bureaucratic web entangling school decision making, it provoked instant UFT-CSA criticism.

Not long before the Bundy report, New York City's central Board of Education had already granted three "demonstration districts" for school decentralization: one in Harlem, another on the Lower East Side, and a third in Brooklyn (Ocean Hill-Brownsville). When principals in these three districts delivered year-end transfer notices to teachers accused by parents of being "racist," the UFT and CSA loudly protested. So even though the UFT had won a compromise solution to the "disruptive clause" problem, it launched renewed teacher walkouts in the fall of 1968.

Many teachers in the three demonstration districts did not honor the strike. Those schools remained open, staffed by the remaining teachers and parent volunteers. On September 30, 1968, the Board of Education granted UFT's demands, including reinstatement of the transferred teachers. Several Ocean Hill-Brownsville principals then declared there was no way they would ever give the "racist" teachers classroom assignments. The Board then suspended the principals, but reinstated them after parent-student protests. This caused the UFT to strike again. Parents, students, and sympathetic teachers, some of them UFT members, once more kept the demonstration district schools open despite severe harassment by strikers, the police, and the courts. Finally, an overall settlement was achieved, and schools reopened on November 19, 1968. But the situation remained tense for years to come.[22]

In the spring of 1969, prominent writer Annette T. Rubinstein, a former New York City school principal, visited P.S. 155 in Ocean Hill-Brownsville. Most of the parents' governing board was black. P.S. 155 was one of the first public schools in New York City to provide a bilingual program (others were P.S. 7 and P.S. 211 in the Bronx).

In the school's bilingual classes Rubinstein observed kindergartners and first graders quickly learning "the three *R*s" in Spanish.[23]

The principal of P.S. 155 was Luis Fuentes, the first Puerto Rican principal ever appointed in New York City. He told Rubinstein: "None of this [bilingual programming] could have taken place, as far as I am concerned, if it were not for this community involvement."[24]

The New York State Legislature passed a new school decentralization law in 1969. Although based on some of the recommendations of the Bundy Committee, the law abolished the three "demonstration districts" and strongly sided with the UFT and the CSA against genuine community control.

In 1970 New York's Latinos faced a tougher battle ahead. That year's national census confirmed what they already knew. Poverty among Puerto Ricans was worse than in 1960. A shocking 47 percent of Puerto Rican students between fourteen and seventeen years old were attending elementary schools. Biased testing and extreme poverty had left Latinos at nearly 30 percent of a New York City school category labeled "educable mentally retarded." Meaningful remedial work was practically nonexistent. School guidance counselors regularly associated Spanish surnames with failure, stamping "Vocational School Recommended" on their record folders even when the contents showed high grade point averages. Not surprisingly, the Puerto Rican school dropout rate surpassed 50 percent. Many experts on education commented that dropping out of school was often a necessary response to an unhealthy or impossible situation. A report by the national Office of Civil Rights added that most who leave before graduating "are bored and find the school unresponsive to their cultural backgrounds, or feel compelled to obtain a job."[25]

Latino parents and students pushed determinedly ahead for school reforms. In 1972 they won a majority in local school board elections for Manhattan's District 1 on the Lower East Side, where three-fourths of public school students were Puerto Rican and the rest mostly African American and Chinese. Luis Fuentes became district superintendent and introduced bilingual and multicultural programs. This led to AFT-CSA moves to oust him. Parents and children launched a prolonged school boycott to secure both Fuentes's job and the new programs.

Although 94 percent of District 1's pupils were nonwhite, 55 percent of the adult population was white, mostly older people residing in housing co-ops, many of them Jewish, Italian, Ukrainian, and Polish Americans. In the school board elections of 1973, their votes, marshaled through a well-financed UFT campaign, gave the UFT-backed slate of candidates a disputed edge over the parents' slate. A federal judge nullified the results on the grounds that the election was "not fairly conducted" and had "discriminatory impact."[26] This was the nation's first election nullified on racial discrimination grounds outside the South.

In 1974, the UFT ran a "Brotherhood" slate listing seventeen white candidates and one black. According to Fuentes, the UFT campaign literature compared the parents' slate to "a magnet for rowdies" and appealed to older Jewish voters by suggesting that "a vote for the Jewish settlement house director who ran on the Parents' Slate was 'a vote for self-hatred'."[27]

UFT leaders, many of them Jewish, had frequently brought charges of "anti-Semitism" against Fuentes and other community control spokespeople. After several lengthy investigations, the charges were dismissed as without basis by the State Commissioner of Education, Schools Chancellor Harvey Scribner, and the State Division of Human Rights. Meanwhile, the UFT-Democratic Party machine won the District 1 elections again, in part because of voter manipulation but also because school-board elections rarely draw much publicity or more than a 10 percent voter turnout. Twenty years later, a special commission found "political coercion and fraud" characteristic of board elections citywide.[28]

Under Fuentes's short-lived leadership of District 1, significant improvements occurred. The city's Addiction Services Agency praised the district's school anti-drug programs, staffed by former addicts, a local priest, and other community workers. Racial and gender imbalances began to be corrected. The number of Spanish-speaking teachers rose from 6 to 120. Out of the district's twenty principals only two had been female before, but five of the new appointees were women. Fifteen vacancies for principals were filled with seven Puerto Ricans, five whites, and three blacks (most of them replaced by pro-UFT whites after the defeat of the Parents' Slate). Bilingual programs were introduced for 6,000 children whose first language was not English, contributing to a big jump in the percentage of children reading at or near grade level.

Looking back on his 1972–1974 tenure as school superintendent, Fuentes noted that these accomplishments were by no means easy ones since community control never really existed under the UFT-backed decentralization law of 1969. That law had led to "the restructuring of the same old failing system behind a new decentralized facade" and "denied to community boards the right to hire and fire pedagogical staff."[29]

Meanwhile, Chicanos were also demanding more control over their classrooms. In cities like Chicago and Milwaukee they sometimes worked in concert with Puerto Ricans. A veritable cultural revolution was affecting youth everywhere, as brilliantly colored and dramatic murals replaced angry graffiti on peeling school and *barrio* walls. Chicano scholarly publications challenged Eurocentric school curricula. *Barrio* theater, dance, music, and art groups sprang up. Latino youths' talents blossomed everywhere, despite the schools—and sometimes to reclaim the schools as rightfully theirs.[30]

A major breakthrough for Chicanos occurred in 1968 with the so-called public school "blowouts" (boycotts, or student walkouts). Apparently, the idea, a very old one (see Chapter 1), popped into the head of a disgruntled teacher, Sal Castro, at Abraham Lincoln High School in one of the East Los Angeles *barrios*. He had been attending community meetings in 1967 that put forward demands for educational reform. A Korean War veteran, he, like Luis Fuentes, had attended college on the GI Bill. As a teacher, he found the racism in the schools disgraceful. The community's mildest demands for reform were routinely ignored, and the Chicano dropout rate was approaching 60 percent. One March morning in 1968 Sal Castro reportedly told his students, "OK, Vamos!" Some one thousand teenagers stormed through Lincoln High's hallways shouting "Blow Out!" Outside on the school lawn they met with parents and other supporters carrying picket signs. Thousands more "blew out" at nearby schools—10,000 by the end of the week! Seventy percent of the student body in five schools honored the boycott. People in the community formed the Educational Issues Coordinating Committee.

The students issued thirty-six demands. They included the hiring of more Latino teachers and counselors; the creation of Latino administrations for schools with majority Latino student bodies; bilingual and bicultural education; smaller classes; improved remedial programs; rehabilitation of non-earthquake-proof buildings; abolition of "homogeneous groupings of students"; "truthful" textbooks; removal of prejudiced teachers and administrators; and "free speech" so that they could discuss the Vietnam War where so many were being sent to fight and die supposedly "to defend free speech" (actually, the U.S.-backed South Vietnamese government was a dictatorship).[31]

The reaction of the Anglo power structure was swift and fierce. Lawmen clubbed student strikers. The FBI blamed a group called the Brown Berets that had originated a year earlier when Chicano young men and women from an interfaith church organization in East Los Angeles had come up with the idea of a community safety patrol.

By 1968, chapters of the Brown Berets (sometimes called Black Berets) existed throughout the Southwest and Midwest. A typical Beret program called for "community control" of schools, "true education of our mestizo culture and Spanish language," "full employment for our people," and "equality for women."[32]

A grand jury indicted thirteen "blowout" leaders, including Sal Castro, on various conspiracy charges. Eleven were members of the Brown Berets or United Mexican American Students (UMAS). Two years later the courts ruled that the charges were unconstitutional. Castro was reinstated.

The harassment eventually led to the breakup of the Brown Berets but not an end to the Chicano struggle for equal education. The flames of the school "blowouts" blew like a prairie fire from *barrio* to *barrio*—Westland near the Mexican border, Santa Clara and Delano to the north, and then eastward to Phoenix, Santa Fe, Denver, San Antonio, Abilene, Chicago, Milwaukee. Gains were made. In Westland's Campbell School, for instance, active community involvement led to a successful bilingual program.[33]

In 1969 thousands of students scraped together enough money to trek to the First National Chicano Youth Liberation Conference in Denver. There they debated and issued El Plan Espiritual de Aztlán (Spiritual Plan of Aztlán—presumed name of the pre-Mexico, pre-U.S. lands). The Plan called for "community control of *barrio* schools." Throughout 1969, Chicano student activists worked with the "traditional" (pre-1960s) Mexican American Political Association (MAPA) to win an election that made Los Angeles's Cucamonga School District the first to come under Chicano control and placed Cucamonga on the Chicano empowerment political map along with Crystal City.

In August 1970 tens of thousands of students and their teachers and parents assembled in Los Angeles for the biggest Latino demonstration ever against the Vietnam War: the "Chicano Moratorium." Unfortunately, as families picnicked at the rally, the police swept the area, clubbing people, overturning baby carriages, and creating a panic. Three were killed during the "police riot."

Despite all of this activity, Latinos continued to be overlooked in the battle to enforce *Brown* and provide for educational equity. They remained the most underrepresented group in school teaching staffs, administrations, and, in many cities, even custodial staff. In 1971 they made up 5 percent of the nation's school population, with 70 percent of them in the Southwest. Only California had started to take official action to correct ethnic imbalances. While the blacks had achieved some school victories in the 1960s, the major advances for Latinos did not come until the 1970s when they were finally recognized as covered by *Brown* and related civil rights legislation.

Latinos continued to push for some "get serious" changes. In 1972–1973, Aspira, assisted by the Puerto Rican Legal Defense and Education Fund, argued a legal case on behalf of 182,000 New York City Spanish-speaking students. It focused on the inequality of educational opportunity caused by language differences. In 1974 the U.S. Supreme Court outlawed English-only instruction in a decision known as *Lau v. Nichols*. The Court ruled that California had violated the "equal protection" clause of the 1964 Civil Rights Act when it deprived children who knew only a little English their rights "to any meaningful education."

After *Lau*, Aspira won a court-supervised "Consent Decree" that obligated New York to provide a massive bilingual-bicultural program with sufficient funding and staff. Although a few changes were made, the Consent Decree, which echoed the recommendations of *The Puerto Rican Study, 1953-1957*, was never carried out. A mid-1980s' report of the National Commission on Secondary Education for Hispanics described the situation "as bad as ever."[34]

In 1974 Congress passed the Equal Educational Opportunity Act, also known as the Bilingual Education

Act, mandating bilingual-bicultural programs. It was much stronger than the 1965 and 1968 acts, whose Title VII it replaced. The 1974 act called for the introduction of bilingual education into ethnically and linguistically mixed classrooms. Its new Title VII declared that children must be allowed to maintain their first language and culture as a means of allowing them "to progress effectively through the educational system."

Based on this and the *Lau* decision, Latinos moved to obtain Aspira-type "consent decree" judgments in several states. They also pushed ahead to win the 1975 Voting Rights Act, which mandated bilingual ballots for districts having more than 5 percent non-English-speaking voters— a major breakthrough that improved Latinos' chances of winning election to school boards.

Unfortunately, bilingual-bicultural programs lagged. Underfunded, they were introduced in less than half the nation's schools. Outright sabotage was common, as happened in 1976 when the U.S. Department of Health, Education, and Welfare sent out a memo stating that bilingual education was not required to provide equal education for non-English-speaking pupils. By the mid-1980s, only 16 percent of "language-minority" fourth graders were receiving any English as second language services at all!

Moreover, bilingual programs in practice usually resulted in a more subtle form of segregation, as Latino children were placed in separate groups or classrooms for language instruction. MALDEF compared the programs in the Southwest to the old "Mexican rooms" in Texas schools. Speakers who spoke little Spanish were often the "bilingual" teachers. Discrimination and humiliation persisted, as confirmed by reports indicating that more than 80 percent of bilingual programs discouraged minority children from using their native languages. As a result, bilingualism and biculturalism came to be viewed by many as a negative force leading to resegregation. Bilingualism-biculturalism, along with *de facto* school segregation, replaced *de jure* segregation as the major educational issues of the day.

As the old residential basis for *de facto* segregation continued, civil rights activists sought new solutions. In 1971 the Supreme Court ruled that "Desegregation plans cannot be limited to the walk-in [neighborhood] school" and that busing could be used to help desegregate schools.[35] Several small-scale race wars erupted over busing. Some nonwhites objected to exposing their children to the difficulties involved.

Many people, including Latino Texans living in San Antonio's poor Edgewood school district (96 percent nonwhite), realized that even if local schools desegregated they would remain unequal because of differences in property tax bases used to calculate school funding. Schools in wealthy suburbs offered their children lavish facilities and well-paid teachers, while poorer schools sometimes were lucky if they had enough chairs, textbooks, blackboards, or chalk. Edgewood itself spent *one-fifteenth* per pupil what a wealthier (white) San Antonio district spent.

Back in March 1968, 400 students had walked out of Edgewood High School to demand equal education. Edgewood's Latino parents had sued in a federal district court to obtain equal school funding. The case, eventually known as *San Antonio Independent School District v. Rodríguez, 1973*, became the nation's pioneering and longest lasting lawsuit against unequal school financing. It is still being fought today and goes to the heart of educational inequities. Its central figure is a retired sheet-metal worker, high school dropout, and son of migrant farmworkers—Demetrio Rodríguez, quoted at the beginning of this chapter.

An initial court ruling in 1971 declared that as a parent of one of the Edgewood schoolchildren Rodríguez had been denied his Fourteenth Amendment right to "equal protection" because the Texas school system was based on local property taxes. That same year Chicanos in an East Los Angeles *barrio* won the important *Serrano v. Priest* ruling that education must be "fiscally neutral." At the same time, a disturbingly racist president, Richard Nixon, was appointing conservative judges to the Supreme Court.[36] Consequently, a 5-to-4 majority on the Supreme Court overturned the Edgewood ruling in *Rodríguez, 1973*. The Court stated that nothing in the U.S. Constitution makes "fiscal neutrality" in education a basic right. Justice Thurgood Marshall could not believe what he was hearing. He asserted that *Brown* clearly made education "a right which must be made available to all on equal terms."[37]

Rodríguez, 1973 left the school funding issue to be worked out by each state or local community. Local court decisions mandated "fiscal neutrality" in education in Texas in 1989, in New Jersey in 1990, and elsewhere, but they were evaded through legal loopholes and tax tinkering. Outright "tax revolts" by middle-class white taxpayers in California and other states led to slashed school budgets that left poorer, predominantly nonwhite schools in even worse conditions. California, with the nation's largest average school class size and the most Latinos, tumbled to forty-sixth in the amount of money budgeted for education.[38]

By the mid-1990s, the differences in school tax bases between urban cores and largely white suburbs had, in fact, widened. Jonathan Kozol, a highly respected expert on public schools, called the classroom results "savage inequalities."

The justice system works slowly, and, as the 1896 *Plessy* and 1973 *Rodríguez* decisions have shown, not always for the best. Demetrio Rodríguez continued to fight his case despite a legacy of hate phone calls and rocks tossed through the windows of his home. In 1989 the Texas Supreme Court decided partially in Rodríguez's favor on technical grounds. Rodríguez won two more court rulings mandating fiscal equalization, but forty-year-old lockers were just starting to be replaced at Edgewood High in 1994. Edgewood students still had a 50 percent dropout rate (four times the national average), and the Rodríguez case dragged on in appellate courts.

Although their victories were never more than partially implemented, Latinos had at last managed to become "visible." The clock could never be turned all the way back. Latinos had become more aware than ever before of the complex problems in education—and how to confront them.

For some, the "into the streets" empowerment movements of the 1960s and early 1970s were the education of their lives. Their participation in "the movements" had not only won bilingual education and increased school enrollments for their children, but had opened the doors to the nation's colleges on a scale few had dreamed possible. Many now stepped through those doors to "reach for the stars."

5
cinco

REACHING

FOR THE STARS

[My teachers] treated me as if I were incapable of learning. . . . It was always hurry up and become Americanized which was idiotic since we were Americans. . . . I had . . . [internalized] their image of me as a loser. By the time I was 12 I was a psychological dropout. . . . [After Army service] I returned to school, graduated and went on to college and graduate school determined to prevent as many Mexican-American students as possible from suffering the same fate that I almost suffered.
> —Anonymous Mexican American
> educator, early 1980s[1]

I felt I had literally crossed a bridge. I could never lead the quiet, respectable life of an academic again, nor did I want to.
> —Dr. Helen Rodriguez, Puerto Rican
> Director of Lincoln Hospital's
> Department of Pediatrics (1970–1974),
> after Young Lords' 1970 takeover of
> the hospital and introduction of child-
> care and "people's health clinics."[2]

The Latinos and African Americans who fought so hard for minority rights thirty years ago scored impressive victories, especially in the field of education. Their enrollments in the nation's colleges more than quadrupled. Many were able to afford college because of the Basic Educational Opportunity Grants program legislated by Congress in 1972 for the economically needy (rebaptized "Pell Grants" eight years later). Currently, more Latino high schoolers than in the past graduate (about 50 percent) and more than a quarter of them go on to college, almost impossible to imagine a few generations earlier.[3]

Despite the victories, Latinos still did not find it easy to attend college, let alone complete their studies. As the Civil Rights Movement receded, it became even more difficult. Inferior high school educations and lack of funds handicapped them. Many had to work full-time while also squeezing in their college work. By 1978 only 32 percent of Chicano males and 15 percent of females who entered college were able to graduate. Then, as scholarships, financial aid, and decent-paying jobs grew more scarce in the 1980s, Latino and African-American college enrollment rates declined, and even fewer completed their studies.[4]

Even worse, in the over-twenty-five age group, 13 percent of all Latinos had less than five years of elementary school—nearly seven times as many as whites and twice as many as African Americans. MALDEF pointed out that the gap between well-educated Latinos and those not even completing grade school reflected a widening gap between haves and have nots in the Latino community, as well as in the entire nation.

Despite their small numbers and so many having to work while they attended school, many of the first Latinos to arrive at the college campuses in the 1960s were active in educational reform movements. Often facing the lack of interest or the opposition of Eurocentric college administrators, they and those who followed them succeeded in creating new programs in Chicano Studies, Puerto Rican and Caribbean Studies, and Latino Studies. Today in California alone there are more than 100 college campuses offering Chicano Studies courses. All California state university campuses offer bachelor's and masters's degrees in Chicano Studies, and two offer the Ph.D. (U.C.-Berkeley and U.C.-San Diego).

Because of the 1960s' push by minorities for equal rights in education, a number of poor white working-class youth also managed to attend college for the first time, taking advantage of the student loan and grant programs won by blacks and Latinos. In the late 1960s new colleges were established to accommodate the influx of applicants. Some elite universities, in order to preserve their upper-class character, opened special campuses for students with lower admission test scores, usually from inner-city ghetto high schools. This was the case, for instance, at Rutgers University, where the multiracial working-class Livingston College campus became noted for the high quality of its faculty and graduates.

Some educational "experts" were surprised that contrary to popular misconceptions about the supersexism of Latino men, known as "machismo," more Latino women than Latino men enrolled and graduated from college (this was true for whites and blacks too). The women's movement had a profound impact on attitudes toward education and careers for women among Latino women. In fact, more Latino than other parents encouraged their daughters' dreams of college.[5]

Among working-class students of both sexes, expecting a chance to go to college is a relatively recent thing. In 1920 there were only about half a million students continuing their education after high school graduation, a far cry from today's estimated fourteen million. Colleges were mainly for the children of the white rich. High school counselors routinely discouraged the educational aspirations of working-class youth. In the 1920s and 1930s, for example, Los Angeles area counselors conducted "surveys of the occupations suitable to and firms employing Negro, Mexican, and Jewish help."[6] An unofficial *de facto* restrictive quota system for entrance into "white" colleges was implemented against Latinos and Jews. Even those who went to college, as part of the tiny allowed quota, were seldom hired to teach on college campuses when they graduated.[7]

Americans did not attend college in large numbers until after the Great Depression and World War II. Prior to that, most of them had to find jobs to contribute to family survival. During the war, workers in the greatly expanded labor unions had agreed not to seek wage hikes as part of the war effort, while most employers had raised prices on goods produced. In 1945–1946, as the war ended, workers went on strike and won significant pay hikes, making it possible for more parents to send their sons and daughters to college.

Having lived through the hard times of the 1930s' Depression, these parents hoped that a college degree would mean a brighter future for the next generation, away from the dull routine of factory production lines. Furthermore, industrial jobs were harder to find with war production ending, and technological changes required a more educated work force. As education historian Sherry Gorelick has pointed out, "working-class communities had to demand access to [college] education with an urgency unprecedented in previous times."[8]

To meet the demand, huge state and community two-year and four-year college systems were built. Initially, most of the students at these low-cost institutions were the male children of unionized white workers—sometimes referred to as "the great American middle class." Relatively few Latinos, at least until the 1960s, survived their daily humiliation in inner-city public schools to even advance to high school. Worse yet, local officials routinely blocked or discouraged admission of Latinos into either high schools or colleges.

A few Latino veterans managed to overcome these obstacles under the GI Bill, a government program giving

World War II and Korean War high-school graduate veterans priority for college admissions and providing a small survival stipend for their expenses. Rodolfo Acuña, who left the Army in 1955, used GI Bill financing to earn a Ph.D. in history at the University of Southern California and went on to found the nation's largest center of Chicano Studies at California State University-Northridge. Others like him helped create Chicano Studies programs on other campuses.

In 1964 a predominantly white "free speech movement" at the University of California-Berkeley made twenty-three-year-old folksinger Joan Baez its bard. The daughter of a Mexican physicist, Baez led students into an administration building to demand the right to have civil rights literature tables on campus.[9] The Berkeley "Free Speech Movement" spread rapidly, as growing numbers of students fought for their constitutional rights to speak out against white racism and the escalating Vietnam War.

Latino activists with experience in the civil rights movement swung into action. Elizabeth ("Betita") Sutherland Martinez, onetime director of the blacks' Student Non-Violent Coordinating Committee (SNCC) office in New York City, became an eloquent voice for all minorities, especially Latinos. In her subsequent career she served as an editor and writer for numerous progressive magazines and journals. Armando Valdez, a SNCC supporter and member of the predominantly white Students for a Democratic Society, launched the Student Initiative at San Jose State College, winning special tutoring for Latinos whose high schools had not adequately prepared them for college.

In 1968 Chicano graduating seniors at San Jose State walked out on the ceremonies with about 200 others, protesting racism on campus. That fall, Latino students, allying with blacks and whites, participated in a much-publicized strike against racism and the Vietnam War at San Francisco State College. The strikers demanded expanded admissions for minority applicants and creation of a Chicano Studies Department. They also supported the strike of the United Farm Workers by calling for an end to the campus's purchase of nonunion grapes. At Berkeley, the Third World Liberation Front conducted similar campaigns.

In the late 1960s, several organizations of Latino college students were launched. One, still active today, was MECHA—El Movimiento Estudiantil Chicano de Aztlán, or Chicano Student Movement of Aztlán. In Santa Barbara, MECHA convened a three-day Chicano conference that issued *El Plan de Santa Bárbara*, a Chicano nationalist manifesto that called on Chicano students and faculty to provide "action-oriented analysis of conditions" and to become "an integral part" of the Chicano community.[10]

In 1970 a group of participants from the Santa Barbara conference published the first issue of *Aztlán: Chicano Journal of the Social Sciences and the Arts*. Its chief editor was Mexico-born UCLA graduate student and poet Juan Gómez-Quiñones, cofounder of UMAS (United Mexican American Students) and later director of UCLA's Chicano Studies Research Center. *Aztlán* sought to uncover the hidden history and dynamic culture of Chicanos "as a colonized people."[11]

Another Chicano journal that made waves at this time was *El Grito: A Journal of Contemporary Mexican American Thought*, a major literary magazine founded by anthropologist Octavio Ignacio Romano-V. and others. Romano-V. also founded the first independent Chicano publishing house, Quinto Sol. It published the first novel of Tomás Rivera, later to be a leading Chicano novelist and first Chicano chancellor of a university research institution (University of California-Riverside). Chicano "activist intellectuals" went on to organize the National Association for Chicano Studies in the mid-1970s.[12]

On the East Coast, Puerto Ricans were involved in similar actions. From 1967 to 1969, students and parents

Shepard Hall, the City College of New York/CUNY

campaigned for an "open admissions" policy at the tuition-free City University of New York (CUNY) campuses.[13] With grassroots community support, Puerto Rican, other Latino, Asian, African-American, and a few white students went on strike and "sat in" at City College. Unknown to the students, CUNY's administration was already planning to open up admissions in the year 1975, but the sit-ins forced speedy action.

As a result, Puerto Rican admissions doubled to 12.6

percent of all admissions by 1970. The CUNY student activists also won the creation of African-American and Puerto Rican studies programs. Numerous journals of distinction were developed by these programs, including CUNY-Hunter's *Bulletin of the Centro de Estudios Puertorriqueños*.

In 1969 New York's Puerto Ricans created the nation's only bilingual college, Eugenio María de Hostos Community College. Located in the South Bronx, the school was named after a famed Puerto Rican advocate of independence. It was headed by Candido de Leon, the first Puerto Rican college president in the United States.

Similar struggles were carried out wherever there was even a handful of Latino college students. At the University of Illinois and other colleges in the Midwest, Puerto Ricans united with Chicanos to launch "sit-ins," demanding open admissions, more Latino teachers, and a greater emphasis on counseling to help newly admitted students stay in school. Their courageous struggles in the face of threats of arrest and expulsion won many concessions, including the creation of the Department of Latin American Studies at the University of Illinois—Chicago Circle Campus.

Older Puerto Rican and Mexican-American educational leaders, while sometimes critical of the empowerment movement's militant tactics, supported the student movement and benefited from it. In 1973 former Aspira leader Antonia Pantoja became chancellor of Washington D.C.'s Universidad Boricua, the nation's only bilingual institution of higher learning controlled by Puerto Ricans.

In 1974 Brooklyn College's popular bilingual education innovator María E. Sánchez, then training prospective schoolteachers, was overlooked by the president when he selected a new head for the Department of Puerto Rican Studies. Four professors and forty students were arrested after occupying the registrar's office in protest. Sánchez was then appointed department head, a position she held until her retirement in 1990.

Latino college activists did not forget the people of their communities. They frequently used campus facilities to extend the struggle for equality into nearby neighborhoods. In 1970, for example, the Young Lords Party and Puerto Rican students held a working conference at Columbia University to help spread the movement and create more day-care centers. The conference was attended by a thousand high-school and college students. In 1971 Latino students helped create Chicago's Spanish Coalition for Jobs and the Latino Institute. All around the country Latino students helped build the successful UFW-sponsored boycott of nonunion grapes and the movement against the Vietnam War.

Latino organizations, like black power groups and those involved in the antiwar movement, were often harassed by the police and the FBI. It took almost two decades, but in 1984 the Spanish Action Community of Chicago won a suit against the Chicago police for its civil rights violations that all but destroyed the organization in 1966. After the mid-1970s, with the demise of the 1960s' movements, activists had to mobilize just to defend their earlier gains (see Chapter 6).

White, black, and Latino women organized their own feminist movements during the late 1960s and early 1970s. Most women involved in the college student movement grew tired of being relegated to secretarial and cooking tasks by male leaders. Although Latinas founded numerous organizations to advance women's equality, comparatively few became "feminist separatists." As noted by Chicana writer Margarita B. Melville, an ex-Maryknoll nun who was a leading anti-Vietnam War activist and is now a University of California-Berkeley professor, Latinas were well aware of their difficult situation of being "twice a minority"—female and nonwhite. They were hesitant to break organizational ties with their Latino "brothers" as long as the racism of white America remained the main obstacle to advancement.[14]

Realizing they were starting from almost ground zero, some Latinos pooled their efforts to found two four-year universities of their own: Washington, D.C.'s Universidad Boricua and National Hispanic University (NHU) in San Jose, California. The founder and president of NHU was Roberto Cruz, who had attended college on a football scholarship. Cruz had noticed that although only 17 percent of African-American students attended black colleges, these schools produced the majority of the small number of black professionals.

SUNY-Albany graduate Angelo Falcón attempted a different approach. In 1982 he founded and became president of the "nonpartisan" Institute for Puerto Rican Policy in New York City. "Our mission," Falcón stated, "is to improve the conditions in our community" by educating politicians and concerned citizens on the "importance of the one-in-four New Yorkers that are Puerto Rican and Latino."[15] In the difficult years ahead, the Institute often exerted its influence on the city's mayors and council members.

After 1972 some Latinos attempting to enter the professions were helped by "affirmative action." That year a Presidential Executive Order instructed employers to take "affirmative action to recruit, employ and promote qualified members or groups formerly excluded."[16] Unfortunately, most employers complied with the order in a tokenistic way. Sometimes, to economize, they sought three minorities for the price of one—a black Latino female!

The majority of new Latino professionals found employment in the fields of social work and education, rather than in higher paying fields like law and medicine. Many worked as bilingual/bicultural teachers and teacher aides. Latino scholars, professors, and writers accounted for only 3.3 percent of the nation's college teachers by 1990. They included major figures like Acuña, Gómez-Quiñones, literature professor Edna Acosta-Belén, historian Virginia Sánchez Korrol, and sociologist Felix Padilla.

As they gained credentials, a significant number of

Latino educators became administrators in heavily Latino school systems. When they proved to be outspoken advocates for the children and teachers of their districts, they were sometimes forced out of their jobs. New York City Schools Chancellor Joseph A. Fernandez was dismissed in the early 1990s when he began implementing state-mandated multicultural programs and introduced AIDS and birth control education.[17]

A combination of a faltering U.S. economy in the 1980s and 1990s and the absence of a mass movement among Latinos slowed down the early gains. Latino teachers and librarians, whether at schools or colleges, never exceeded 3.5 percent of the total number. The percentage of Latino educational and vocational school counselors stood at only 5 percent in 1990. In 1994 New York City school officials acknowledged that there was even a lack of Latino personnel among custodial staff. Even as bilingual teachers, Latinos are still underrepresented, although an estimated 200,000 more will be needed by the year 2000.

Latinos comprised less than 3.5 percent of the nation's social scientists and urban planners (and only 7 percent of the social workers) in 1990. This often helped to maintain a vicious cycle of racism that prevented more Latinos from entering those fields. An earlier investigation of the social sciences revealed that white scholars dominating the field rarely presented "an excellent or even adequate portrayal" of Latinos.[18]

Most professional jobs are given to graduates with traditionally accepted majors. Yet those are the very college departments most likely to exclude Latinos. One researcher has discovered that minorities are often "shut out" or "marginalized" into poorly funded and sometimes ridiculed "academic slums and backwaters with names like Afro-American studies."[19]

In other professions, the story of relative Latino exclusion is similar.[20] On average, Mexicans and Central Americans are at the bottom of the Latino heap since

Joseph A. Fernandez, former New York City schools chancellor

Cubans and Puerto Ricans have higher participation rates in the professions than they do.[21]

Inequities in graduate education are a large part of the problem. Professional schools still tend to exclude Latinos. In 1985 Latino enrollments were universally 3 percent or less in dentistry, law, medical, and engineering schools.[22] To help confront the problem, Latino professionals, not forgetting the difficulties they had experienced, formed numerous organizations like the Society of Hispanic Professional Engineers or the Association of Mexican American Educators.

Some of the obstacles to success were bluntly described

Ramon C. Cortines, successor to
Fernandez as schools chancellor

in the report of a 1985 conference of medical school deans
and presidents:

> *[Because of] the brutal reality of money, a major*
> *barrier for minority students is a substandard general*
> *education, from an early age, culminating in poor*
> *quality science teaching in some high schools and even*
> *in some colleges.*

One of the deans recommended radical surgery—"changing the total educational system."[23]

Brooklyn-born Hostos College president Isaura

Santiago, a veteran of Aspira, candidly acknowledged that she switched her major from science to liberal arts when she realized her "ghetto schooling left me unprepared for the tough competition."[24] New York City's newly appointed chancellor of education, Ramon C. Cortines, vowed in 1994 to do something about the inadequate science and math education being offered that city's predominantly nonwhite students.[25]

Latinos have also been shut out of the top echelons of the mass media, although there are many Spanish-language publications and radio and TV programs. Concludes Raul Yzaguirre, president of the National Council of La Raza, a lobbying umbrella group representing 150 community-based organizations:

> *we have simply gone from being completely invisible to being a token. . . . But with the Endowment for the Humanities, the Corporation for Public Broadcasting, the media in general, and the business roundtable, we are not even a token.*[26]

When all else fails, it is tempting for young Latinos to dream of becoming "superstars" in entertainment, the arts, or sports, where natural talent is sometimes the entry ticket to fame. Some have gone on to succeed in these worlds. But all too often expensive training and upscale connections are as important as inborn talent. Only a few Latinos from the working class, through good grades and scholarships, have worked their way through highly competitive schools of music, dance, theater, film making, and art to achieve successful careers.[27]

In art, a surprising number of Latino teenage muralists, some of them high school "pushouts," have gone on to gain stature among art connoisseurs and historians. This has happened despite their near-total exclusion from the "official art world." A national task force appointed by Washington D.C.'s prestigious Smithsonian Institution reported in 1994 that the Smithsonian had "virtually ignored Hispanic contributions to American art, culture and science" and shown "a pattern of willful neglect."[28]

Latino novelists and poets abound. Most communicate powerful messages of human courage and love in the face of adversity, but they are little known outside of Latino circles. Puerto Rican novelist Nicholosa Mohr's sensitive, moving works for young adults have inspired many to push ahead despite the barriers. A few "Nuyorican" poets (Puerto Ricans raised in New York) have gained modest recognition. One, Pedro Pietri, typifies Latino anger and humor in poems like "Suicide Note for a Cockroach in a Low Cost Housing Project."

In the business world too Latinos are grossly underrepresented. Even though Latinos have a purchasing power approaching 200 billion dollars, their many talented entrepreneurs are excluded from the senior ranks of large corporations. White males hold 96 percent of top management positions; Latino males hold 0.7 percent; and Latino females 0.1 percent. On the other hand, the number of Latino small businesses nearly doubled during the 1980s. Like other small businesses, Latino enterprises frequently fail. Occasionally, by filling a special niche market, Latino entrepreneurs do well. In 1969, for example, Jesús Chavarría, editor of the Chicano-nationalist *El Plan de Santa Bárbara*, started a new slick magazine, *Hispanic Business*.

In the world of politics, where the power to change laws resides, Latinos are even more underrepresented, lagging far behind African Americans. In 1990 they filled less than one percent of the nation's half million elected posts.[29]

A little known fact is that the largest number of Latino "professionals" fall at or below the poverty line. That is because many jobs labeled "professional" pay little more than manual labor. The rapidly growing, four-million-strong field of "allied health professionals," for example, includes not only workers requiring advanced training like physical therapists but jobs for nurses' aides and orderlies that pay barely enough for survival. Latina and African-American women, categorized as allied health professionals, often do the lowest paid work at public hospitals, nursing homes, outpatient facilities, and clinics.

School "tracking" remains a stubborn problem for would-be Latino professionals. In 1980 only 25 percent of Latino high school students were in academic tracks, 40 percent were in general tracks, and the remaining 35 percent were slotted into vocational programs. Less than a third of the vocational graduates were able to find work in the trades they studied.

More than a third of the 1980s' Latino and black high-school graduates received failing grades in the core academic subjects of mathematics, natural science, social science, and English, compared with about 10 percent of white graduates. Under the accumulated burdens of tracking, poor teaching and counseling, and fear of failure, only 28 percent of Latino high school seniors took the SATs (standardized college entrance tests).[30]

More than one researcher has concluded that the SATs are "racist," since Latino scores notably improve whenever language, class, and cultural references on the tests are revised to incorporate Latinos. The SATs supposedly predict college success. The scores of Latinos are lower than those of whites, but Latinos who attend college do far better than their SAT scores would indicate.

Even when they do well on the SATs, Latinos are discouraged from going to college. Recalls Guillermo Vasquez, New York State Department of Correctional Services Education Supervisor:

> *Although my SAT scores were high enough to be accepted to a variety of universities, my counselor told me I would never make it in college and should start looking for a job. (I later found out she had already convinced some of my friends not to attend college even though their scores were also high enough.) Some years later I saw her at a Christmas concert at that same school. I wondered how many more Chicanos*

*she had managed to convince to give up. I wanted to
tell her that I had graduated from the University of
Texas at Austin, had gotten a scholarship to study in
Latin America and was now working on my Master's
Degree. Maybe even thank her . . . for infuriating me
and making me even more determined to prove she
was very wrong.* [31]

Many recommendations by educators to improve the
teaching of Latinos are ignored for many years. As early as
1972 the American Association of Colleges for Teacher
Education called for teacher training in "cultural diversity," "alternative and emerging life styles," and "multiculturalism, multilingualism." [32] Yet by 1990 few prospective
schoolteachers were taking even one multicultural education
class, making it difficult if not impossible for them to teach
successfully in urban, ethnically mixed schools.

Appearance, rather than capability, is still all too often
an important factor in success. A disproportionate number of those Latinos who succeed in "reaching for the stars"
are white—if not in skin pigmentation, then in cultural
stance. A case in point is Richard Rodriguez, whose widely
publicized and read autobiography, *Hunger of Memory,* made
him a favorite speaker on the lecture circuit in the 1980s.

Subtitled "The Education of Richard Rodriguez," the
book tells of how this middle-class brown-skinned Mexican
American "made it" in the white world and then became
torn by guilt and shame at his own abandonment of the
warm, loving, friendly world of his "Mexican" family.
Rodriguez remembers how, as a boy, he tried to shave off his
dark skin with a razor blade. When his mother stopped
using Spanish in the home to satisfy a teacher's wishes, he
became confused and angry. He corrected his parents'
English, confessing "I was not proud of my mother and
father." [33] Through hard work and private tutoring paid for
by his parents, he became exceptionally proficient in
English. In his autobiography he says he went on to become
culturally "white"—but at the cost of great psychic harm.

Rodriguez, a self-described "scholarship boy" and

"Ph.D. professor," honestly recognizes he never would have succeeded had it not been for the civil rights movement. But in his biography he criticizes bilingualism and affirmative action for creating "an elite society," claiming that the "least disadvantaged were helped first." He denounces Chicano civil rights activists for pushing "to get more nonwhite students into colleges" when the "revolutionary demand would have called for a reform of primary and secondary schools."[34]

Actually, many activists demanded and continued to call for reforms of the entire educational system. Rodriguez's book confirms what too often happens when Latinos in schools and colleges attempt to "de-Latinize" in order to conform to white expectations.[35] A leading historian, Mario García, has concluded that the "historical amnesia of the 1980s" exemplified by Rodriguez's *Hunger of Memory* must be replaced by "a memory of history—a history of uncompromising dedication and struggle for full equality with other Americans."[36]

Unfortunately, the goals of the "Reagan Revolution" were very different.

6
seis

BACKLASH!

There has been an across-the-board breakdown in the machinery that six previous administrations constructed to protect civil rights.
—Arthur Fleming, former director,
U.S. Civil Rights Commission[1]

There has been a massive failure of public schools to educate poor children and children of color. Most public schools are boring, lifeless places that serve a few students well, push most through, and get rid of or stigmatize students who become identified as "problems."
—Widely published educational expert
Herbert Kohl, 1989[2]

[Equal opportunity is a] myth that rationalizes hierarchy, justifies disproportionate access to goods and power, and shames those at the bottom into internalizing inadequacy.
—Legal scholar Alan Freeman, 1988[3]

They [put me in a work program] cleaning toilets at a recreational center. . . . [I'm] somebody with a college education. If they put me in that job . . . imagine what they'd do to some guy who dropped out of school.
—Joe Vasquez, Puerto Rican college
graduate, 1992[4]

In reaction to the movements of the 1960s and 1970s, a "white backlash" and "male backlash" spread across the nation.[5] It contributed to the rise inside the Republican Party of the "New Right," whose most persuasive spokesperson was telegenic movie actor and radio commentator Ronald Reagan, twice elected to the presidency in the 1980s.

The backlash provided public support for the "Reagan revolution" and its deregulation of the economy and nonenforcement of civil rights laws. As part of the rise of the New Right, conservative Latino spokespeople gained a strong voice—individuals like Linda Chavez, head of the U.S. Civil Rights Commission under President Reagan. Chavez's book *Out of the Barrio* championed the uninformed myth of "they made it why can't you?" (see Chapter 1). The presidencies of Reagan and his vice president George Bush (1990–94) slashed budgets for education, bilingual programs, and even for Head Start, which now serves less than a third of prekindergarten children who qualify and for less time than the original program. Financial aid for college attendance by Latinos and blacks plummeted, as the Reagan administration eliminated the two-billion-dollar Guaranteed Student Loan Program. By 1986 the percentage of Latino high-school graduates going on to college had dropped to 29 percent from a high point in 1976 of 36 percent.

The white backlash caused many ugly episodes on college campuses. According to a 1990 estimate by a spokesman for the National Institute Against Prejudice and Violence, one of every five minority students attending predominantly white colleges experienced "assaults, vandalism, or verbal harassment motivated by racial prejudice." Ironically, some of the racial incidents on campuses in 1993–1994 pitted small numbers of black and Jewish students against one another at a time when minorities needed to unite more than ever.[6]

The administration of President Bill Clinton (1993–) initially reversed only a few of the anti-minority measures of the "Reagan revolution," such as forbidding abortion counseling in federally funded clinics. In matters of education, it proposed new student loan programs but failed to restore all the budget cuts in federal aid to education. The president signed a paltry one-billion-dollar education package in 1994.

Many writers and educators compared the white backlash to the backlash in the South that produced the "black codes" and the Jim Crow laws following the period of Reconstruction. Both the Ku Klux Klan and a "neo-Nazi" movement advocating WASP supremacy began to operate openly in the 1980s, running candidates for office. After launching KKK armed patrols of the Mexican border in the name of helping the INS prevent illegal immigration, Klan leader David Duke won a seat in the Louisiana legislature in 1989. He went on to campaign for the Republican presidential nomination.

New genetics-type arguments reminiscent of the early 1900s' eugenics movement also surfaced. An author of psychological tests for schoolchildren wrote a book in 1987 that asserted "the probability that inherited genetic material is a contributing factor" to low scores of Puerto Ricans and Mexican Americans on intelligence tests.[7] A widely publicized 1994 book, *The Bell Curve*, claimed that low IQ test scores "prove" the intellectual inferiority of African Americans and that IQ is a largely inherited function. Worse yet, the federal government funded a multimillion-dollar research project called the "violence initiative." It aimed to identify potentially violent inner-city children based on biological and genetic "markers" in order to treat "vulnerable" children and youth with psychiatric drugs tested on Rhesus monkeys. [8]

The Supreme Court's new conservative majority rendered several 5-to-4 rulings that reinforced the backlash and helped resegregate the nation's schools. From *Milliken v. Bradley, 1975* to *Board of Education v. Dowell, 1991*, the Court dealt lethal blows to the use of busing for the purposes of desegregation. *Milliken, 1975* exempted suburban schools altogether, while *Dowell, 1991* returned all school districts to local control on the grounds that "economics" was the cause of continued segregation. Justice Thurgood Marshall pointed out that this decision struck down the basic premise of *Brown*: that, whatever the reason, "separate educational facilities are inherently unequal."[9]

Perhaps the crowning blow was *The Regents of the University of California v. Bakke, 1978.* The Court ruled five-to-four that the UC-Davis Medical School's affirmative action program for assuring admission of nonwhites had unlawfully denied admission to white student Allan Bakke, whose test scores were higher than those of sixteen nonwhites admitted under the program. The majority said that Bakke's civil rights had been violated. In their dissents, justices Harry Blackmun and Marshall declared that the *Bakke* decision struck at the heart of the implementation of *Brown*. Affirmative action, they said, was obviously necessary if racial inequalities were ever to be corrected. Marshall added that just as *Brown* had reversed *Plessy*, so now *Bakke* reversed *Brown*.

The Supreme Court also waffled on affirmative action cases in areas other than education. As a *New York Times* editorial on April 28, 1994, pointed out, the Court's decisions "so muddled the legal rules for job discrimination cases that Congress had to pass [the 1991 Civil Rights Act] . . . to restore the force of long-standing former laws." Then, by refusing to apply the 1991 act to cases pending when it was enacted, the Court "left thousands of people out of court."[10]

In other words, not only were laws against racially discriminatory practices not being implemented—cases were not even being heard! Vast numbers of Latinos, of course, could not afford the costs of a court case to begin with. Legal scholars concluded that the federal courts had developed a "multitier" approach to protecting people's rights. At the lowest unprotected tier were such rights as education, housing, job fairness, and basic human welfare—the concerns most important to minority groups suffering discrimination.

With busing basically eradicated, educational inequity became more tied to housing patterns than ever before. In housing, Latinos are now the nation's most discriminated-against group. A 1991 report by the Department of Housing and Urban Development found that Latinos seeking to buy or rent homes or apartments experienced discriminatory treatment at least half the time. This "redlining" to preserve the racial composition of a neighborhood had been outlawed for decades. Its illegal continuation further undermined Latinos' chances for a quality education.[11]

According to the 1990 census, 45 percent of all Americans live in suburbs, 95 percent of them white. Suburbanization is a way of "sorting out winners and losers."[12] It leaves inner cities with a lower tax base for education. A suburban public school typically spends twice as much on each student as an urban one. In the words of New York State Education Commissioner Thomas Sobol, there are "two distinct types of school systems—one urban, minority, poor, and failing, and the other suburban, white, affluent, and successful."[13] Even in the suburbs, the majority of Latinos and African Americans attend segregated schools in special housing developments built for minorities.

By the mid-1990s, Latinos were society's most segregated group of students after Native Americans—73 percent of them attended classes with predominantly nonwhite students. Latinos were more segregated in California and Texas than blacks were in Mississippi and Alabama. New York State ranked first in school segregation for both Latinos and blacks.[14]

As segregation increased, conditions and academic standards in most public schools declined, leading to higher national rates of illiteracy. Functional illiteracy was first noted by employers in emerging industries who found their new employees unable to perform simple reading and arithmetic tasks. A 1975 study found 56 percent of Latinos functionally illiterate in English compared with 44 percent of blacks and 16 percent of whites. In 1983, the National Commission on Excellence in Education warned: "Our Nation is at risk." Jonathan Kozol's books *Prisoners of Silence, Illiterate America,* and *Savage Inequalities* further alerted the nation.

Then *The National Education Goals Report: 1993* announced that nearly half of the nation's adults were functionally illiterate. Only 13 percent of adults could identify the main argument in a newspaper article, and only 14 percent could use a bus schedule or calculate percentages for a restaurant tip. Less than a quarter of fourth, eighth, and twelfth graders were meeting performance standards for grade level in math and reading. Writing and science skills were in decline. Even among the most "educationally advantaged," less than 5 percent could understand scientific materials or historical documents. Taking into account the costs of unemployment, health care, welfare, and incarceration, it was said that illiteracy cost the nation up to 200 billion dollars annually. Industry lost in productivity and competitiveness.

Educators referred to the "Matthew effect" in literacy—"the rich become richer and the poor become poorer." Kozol called it "the cycle of illiteracy." The human cost was in fact immeasurable, as a "competence gap" between haves and have-nots stretched ever wider. With technology's frequent changes, three-fourths of the labor force needed complete retraining every seven to ten years—and neither big business nor the school system seemed willing to absorb the costs.[15]

By the early 1990s, four out of every five new jobs required more than a high-school education—in other words, advanced education or training. Meanwhile, among the twenty-to-twenty-four age group, 40 percent of Hispanics, 23 percent of African Americans, and 17 percent of whites had never graduated from high school. A lesser percentage of Latinos than either African Americans or whites were entering or completing college or graduate school, placing them further behind in the job market competition.

In the face of these harsh realities, there developed signs of growing Latino hopelessness. The Latino school dropout rate rose a few points in the 1980s. Worse yet, the dropout rates were in reality much higher than those reported. Many Latinos were classified as attending school on the basis of an occasional presence in class or of their stated intent to take the GED high school diploma equivalency exam. Aspira announced in 1983 that the real dropout rates ran as high as 72 percent for African Americans and 80 percent for Hispanic students in New York State. By 1984, half of the nation's Latinos fourteen and fifteen years of age were officially classified as "at risk" (either not enrolled or at least one grade level behind), compared with 25 percent of "at risk" non-Latinos.[16]

A major reason Latinos dropped out was the declining value of a high-school diploma. Latino high school graduates did not earn much more than those without diplomas. A 1981 study for the National Council on Education Statistics found that Puerto Rican dropouts actually had a better chance of getting a job than Puerto Rican high-school graduates. Researchers noted that for each year of school completed the economic return for Latinos was not nearly as great as it was for non-Latinos. Of all Latino families with members who had completed four years of high school, 16 percent lived in poverty in 1988—up from 12.5 percent a decade earlier.

Some Latinos believed that if a diploma would not bring better job possibilities, there was little point in remaining in boring and dangerous high schools. A four-year study for the New York Board of Education concluded that making classes more appealing for students was the most important change to make to lower dropout rates. A Chicago study added that violence in the schools, a sense of hopelessness, and teenage pregnancies were important reasons for students' leaving.

There is no denying that schools in many cities and even some suburbs are becoming unsafe. A survey of New York State schools in 1993 found that one in five students brings a knife, gun, or some other weapon to school. Twenty percent of the students and 8 percent of the teachers say they experience at least one assault during the school year. Half the students complain about classroom disruptions interfering with their learning. A tough "law and order" approach of "turning school into disciplinary barracks" by distributing handcuffs to city schools clearly is not working.[17]

Today the majority of Latinos are not receiving a genuine high-school education. Many languish in so-called "special ed" classes, for which the criteria are often vague or racially discriminatory. Secretary of Education Richard S. Riley asks: "Could it be that [in] our attempt to do good—offering pullout programs and overlabeling students into special education classes—we have contributed [to] . . . racial stereotyping that tells these young people early on that they will not make it in life, so why even try?"[18]

In Hartford, Connecticut, television reports in 1994 revealed that gangs were appearing among Latino grade school students because no one among the adults in the schools seemed to care about them. For youth of any age from broken homes, the gangs serve as substitute families. Gang members or other youth who "deal drugs" are often making more money than the income from a low-paid job or a welfare check.[19]

The escalating white backlash, the regressive Supreme Court decisions, the rising illiteracy and dropout rates, and the growth of gangs all happened at a time when the economy was stumbling from recession to recession. Millions of white "middle-class" automotive, steel, and other workers were dismissed from their jobs. The economic crisis and job market changes of the 1990s started two decades earlier, when the government poured billions of dollars down the bottomless hole of the Vietnam War and large corporations accelerated their move overseas to hire inexpensive cheap labor and to avoid new antipollution laws.

Economic changes have divided the nation into a "two-tiered society" dominated by a relatively small number of well-off, mostly white people.[20] In the 1980s, the richest 1 percent of Americans doubled their purchasing power. By 1990, the combined income of the top one-fifth of the population surpassed that of the remaining four-fifths. Not surprisingly, most of the children from the upper income group attended private schools.

A 1994 report issued by the Department of Labor and the Commerce Department said that society was becoming polarized into one of "haves and have-nots." It warned that the ongoing wage gap "between white and nonwhite workers" would likely spell an end to social stability and democracy.[21]

Today, depending on which statistics are used, from 18 to 40 percent of people with full-time jobs earn less than the extremely low "poverty level" set by the government for a family of four. Most families have two breadwinners. More than half of young adults ages eighteen to twenty-four are still living at their parents' homes, some enrolling in hometown, state-supported two-year colleges while working odd jobs.

The 1990 Census shows only a tenth of whites as "poor," compared with 40.6 percent of Puerto Ricans, 31.9 percent of African Americans, and 28.1 percent of all Latinos. Employed African Americans earn more than Latinos, but blacks suffer higher unemployment rates. Even among Latino groups doing better—the Cubans for example—growing numbers of families are poor. Today, more than forty million Americans go hungry; twenty-three million depend on food stamps; and up to seven million are homeless. More than a million children are homeless, and at least twelve million children suffer frequent hunger. Some

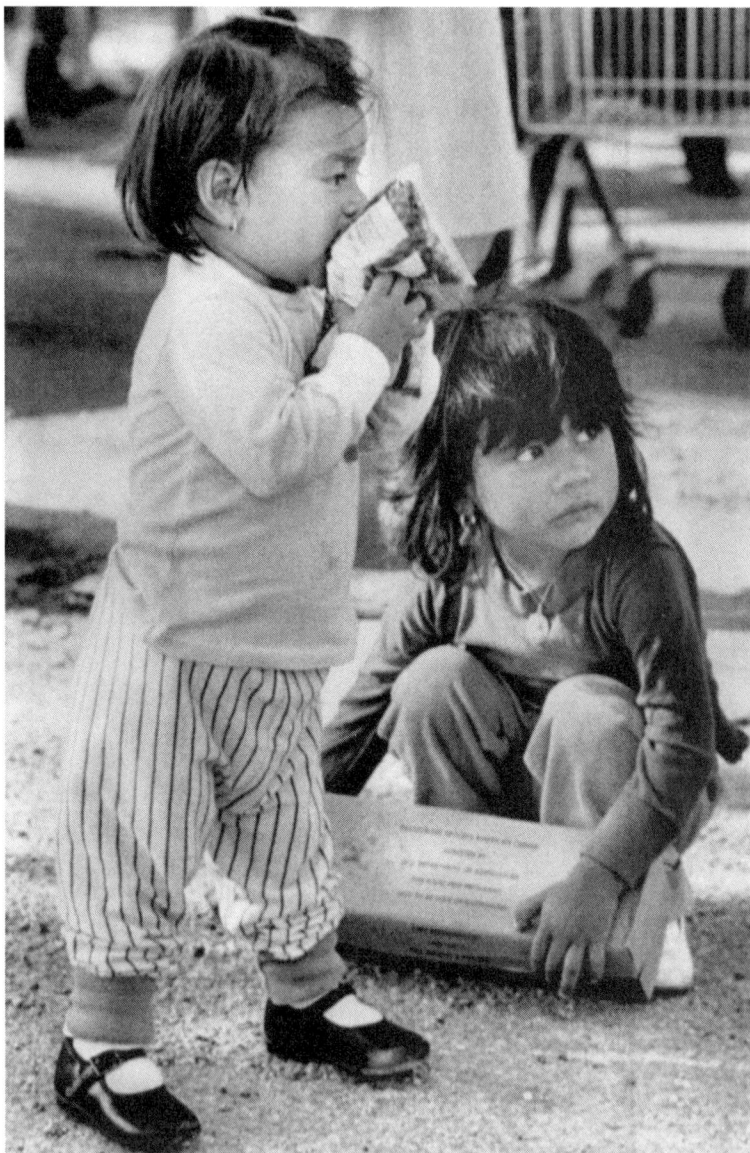

These Latino children of an unemployed
farmworker hold a bag of black beans and a block
of cheese their mother received at Centro-
Campesino, a social service office in Homestead,
Florida, for migrant workers and their families.

39 percent of Latino children and half of black children live in poverty. This stark picture is made worse each day by recent reductions in budgets for school lunches.

Latina and black women and their children are the hardest hit. Close to 30 percent of the nation's births are to single parents. Unable to find decent jobs or day-care for their children, most of them find it necessary to receive welfare payments within four years of giving birth. Their conditions have become desperate. Welfare benefits for a parent and two children have been slashed more than a third since 1972 to less than $8,000 a year and to only $3.75 a day for a new baby (or in some states, zero dollars). One-fifth of Mexican American families and two-fifths of Puerto Rican ones are female-headed. Latina women account for over 21 percent of the nation's AIDS cases.[22]

Politicians talk of ending welfare and putting people back to work, but they realize that the expenses of day-care and literacy-plus-job training far exceed welfare costs. Moreover, critics ask, with millions of people already unemployed, where would welfare mothers find work?

The picture is grim not just for Latinos and blacks. It threatens the future prosperity of all Americans. New entrants into the workforce through the year 2000 are expected to be 85 percent minorities and women. Latinas are already entering the labor force at twice the rate of non-Latino U.S. women. The U.S. Bureau of the Census projects that by the year 2000 young people of Mexican descent will be second only to young whites as the largest source of new workforce entrants. In other words, today's Latino children are a big part of tomorrow's workforce. Latino men and women, many of them recent immigrants, are already fundamental for the functioning of the economy (see Chapter 7).[23]

There may be more jobs for Latinos, but few of the jobs are desirable. The U.S. Bureau of Labor Statistics points out that there will be an increase of approximately 250,000 computer systems analysts between 1986 and 2000 but more than 2.5 million jobs for waiters, waitresses, chambermaids and doormen, clerks, and custodians.[24] Student use of computers is more common in predominantly white schools than in segregated ones, which further helps to track Latinos toward the worse jobs.

Throughout the current period of the white backlash and slashed education budgets, Latinos have been fighting back. In Mendota, a small farm town in California's Central Valley, concerned parents discovered that a thousand children of migrant workers were not receiving bilingual instruction even though the school was receiving monies for that purpose and had built up a ten-million-dollar school budget surplus. A U.S. Department of Education report found that the youngsters' civil rights had been violated. It quoted one teacher as saying she had "no idea" if students even understood the subject matter since she did not speak Spanish. The parents formed Adelante Mendota (Forward Mendota). They obtained enough signatures to force a recall election for five of seven school board members. Their candidates then won all five seats and introduced changes to upgrade the school's performance. Similar struggles involving student boycotts of classes and voter registration drives occurred in California's San Joaquin Valley.[25]

In Chicago, Latinos supported a new "rainbow" coalition that twice elected African-American reform Democrat Harold D. Washington mayor. Realizing their votes were Washington's "margin of victory" in 1983, Latinos pressured the mayor to do something about the wretched schools. They launched peaceful marches and religious liturgies to protest a report by the Chicago Board of Education that underestimated the number of school dropouts. Many among the city's million resident Latinos joined the school reform movement led by rank-and-file members of the mayor's "rainbow" coalition and supported by concerned business executives. It radically changed the city's schools, turning them over to parent-teacher councils. Concerned educators contributed their talents by organizing TAMS

(Teachers' Academy of Mathematics and Science). The children's advocacy group Design for Change promoted the Chicago movement and now works in other schools districts around the nation.[26]

In the late 1980s and early 1990s, parents in a multiracial Milwaukee neighborhood mobilized to save a ninety-year-old school building and convert it into a model bilingual elementary school. Despite the Milwaukee School Board's stubborn opposition, the parents won a prolonged struggle that produced "La Escuela Fratney," a successful kindergarten-through-five grade school housed in the old building. With 350 students, of whom 60 percent are Latino, the school has become a national model for bilingual and multicultural education.[27]

In Los Angeles, Latinos organized to elect Latinos to the city council and local school boards, after more than a century of exclusion. One of the first to be elected to the city's Board of Education was Leticia Quezada, the daughter of a Mexican copper miner. Quezada believes that since the children of noncitizens attend school, their parents should have the right to vote in school board elections. She called for more bilingual programs, perhaps remembering her own arrival to the United States when she dropped from a straight A average in Mexico to failing grades in California. Attacked by critics for only having an interest in Latino children, she countered: "I think all the children should be bilingual . . . in this . . . multicultural nation." Elected president of the Board in the early 1990s, she came under fire for her methods of enforcing budgetary cuts through severe salary reductions instead of layoffs for teachers.[28]

In New York, parents almost rioted when they learned in 1993 that city inspectors had failed to report dangerous levels of cancer-causing asbestos in school buildings. After being shut down, repaired, and reopened, some buildings in the poorest neighborhoods were again found to be unsafe. Parents and children in Brownsville and East New York, most of them Latinos and African Americans, organized mass protest marches demanding safe, well-equipped schools.

College students also have been fighting back. In New York, when authorities tried to eliminate the recently founded Hostos College, Latino students occupied campus buildings and conducted mass marches to City Hall. Their determined show of support for the college saved it from infanticide.

New York's CUNY students organized against the 1975 introduction of tuition and the steep tuition hikes that followed. The rising costs cut into the percentage of Latino graduates from the CUNY system—only 11 percent by 1981. Then, in the early 1990s, tuition nearly doubled to $2,450; state aid plummeted by $200 million; and CUNY cut its staff by 17 percent. This not only undermined the quality of a CUNY degree—it made it impossible for poorer students to continue their education. Latino and black students, sometimes joined by poor white ones, held sit-ins and rallies for weeks at a time. CUNY campuses shut down. The administration suspended several students, and the campuses reopened. The struggle was weakened but not killed.

Latino students at CUNY's Hunter College and New York's Latino community went on to mobilize a campaign to overturn the college president's refusal to appoint Dr. María Canino director of the famous Centro de Estudios Puertorriqueños. A former member of CUNY's Board of Trustees who had long defended minority students' rights, Canino had the unanimous recommendation of a CUNY-wide search committee. Canino had left the Trustees to direct the prestigious Puerto Rican Studies Department at Livingston College of Rutgers University (see Chapter 5), where she remained as a tenured professor. Livingston's original pro-minorities mission had been gutted by budget cuts and tuition hikes. In 1994 Hunter's president left for another job, leaving the Centro without a director for at least two years. [29]

Throughout the 1980s and 1990s, Latino and other students launched similar mass direct actions throughout the nation. San Francisco State University's Progressive Student Coalition, led by nonwhite students, won the student government elections for ten consecutive years. It hosted a national conference convened in 1992 by the National People of Color Student Coalition.

Campus protests were not limited to "defensive" actions. Student activists also sought admissions policies more reflective of local ethnic composition and greater attention to Latino and other minority issues.[30] They demanded improvements in the quality of their education and a broader curriculum reflecting the multinational and multicultural character of U.S. history, society, and literature.

At UCLA, where 11 percent of the students are Mexican American, students and faculty conducted a series of rallies, sit-ins, and a hunger strike that won the elevation of the Chicano Studies program to the status of a regular department. Only two other campuses could claim this distinction—University of California-Santa Barbara and California State University-Northridge. At Michigan State University (MSU), Latinos formed a coalition with Asian-American students to demand Chicano and multicultural studies programs there. At high-tuition Stanford, a "rainbow coalition" of mostly minority students occupied the president's office, helping to bring about the 1991 introduction of a new required "diversity" course incorporating the works of blacks, Hispanics, feminists, and homosexuals.

Many campuses refused such demands on the false grounds that there were not enough "qualified" faculty. According to UCLA's Antonio Serrata, assistant director of the Chicano Studies Research Center, "The universities just don't want to hire the faculty, and some of that has to do with racism and difference in ideology."[31]

The white backlash targeted Latino faculty members who were politically active or spoke out for multiculturalism.

In the early 1990s, conservatives at the University of California-Santa Barbara, including a faculty member who reportedly had worked for the CIA, sabotaged the appointment of famed labor historian Rodolfo Acuña as the campus's first full-time permanent Chicano Studies professor. Thousands of students throughout the state rallied to demand Acuña's hiring. Scholars from around the nation expressed their indignation. The American Civil Liberties Union, the Center for Constitutional Rights, and the National Coalition for Universities in the Public Interest concluded that the denial of Acuña's appointment was based on political grounds and constituted a civil rights violation. A team of fifteen pro-bono lawyers took the case to court, where it still awaits resolution. Acuña said that any monies accruing to him from the case would be donated to a foundation for Chicanos in higher education.

The defensive struggle to combat racism and maintain educational gains, like the offensive one to improve educational opportunity and quality and to hire more Latino faculty, seemed at times a losing battle. The State University of New York system, for example, doubled its tuition in two years (1991–93). The alternative of attending a private college wasn't a possibility for most Latinos because of even higher costs. Budget cuts in California led to severe reductions in openings at state colleges—159,000 fewer admissions in the 1993–94 academic year—most of them at two-year campuses previously attended by Latinos.

Because of escalating costs and reduced budgets, the sun was setting on the era of mass education at the very moment it seemed to be rising on the era of multiculturalism. Yet in the practice of coalition building and fighting back, Latinos were learning—and teaching—the lesson that students have more power than they may realize. In the words of MSU biochemistry professor Diana Martinez: "Students have a lot of unused power, and they have to learn how to be involved more and use it more effectively. No university can survive without students and their input."[32]

7
siete

IN MY OWN

TONGUE

It's frustrating. I'm stuck in menial work because I don't speak English, and I don't speak English because I can't afford to quit my menial jobs to take a class.
> —Juliana Loma, immigrant from
> Panama, 1993[1]

[Bilingual education is] a basic democratic right of our community, a pedagogically sound approach, which provides equal opportunity to a large segment of the university's future population.
> —Dr. Maria J. Canino, member of CUNY
> Board of Higher Education, 1986[2]

*They pray in Spanish to an Anglo God with a Jewish heritage. . . .
all fervently hoping
that if not omnipotent,
at least He be bilingual.*
> —Judith Ortiz Cofer, 1987[3]

To devalue a minority child's language is to devalue the child.
> —James Crawford, 1994[4]

The color of America's face radically changed in the 1980s, as some 8.6 million new immigrants arrived, most of them Latinos and Asians. Racial purists feared the "de-whitening" of America, and bilingual education in the public schools became the center of a raging controversy. The U.S. Census Bureau projected that by the year 2000, Hispanics would comprise one-fourth of the population and that by 2030, a majority of U.S. residents would be non-white.[5]

In some places "immigrant bashing" became fashionable, and racial tensions were heightened. Journalists described the nation's 2,000-mile-long border with Mexico, for example, as a "war zone." Some members of the U.S. Border Patrol were accused of shootings, beatings, and other abuses of "illegals."[6] In San Diego County, a few teenagers shot at Mexican immigrant workers "for sport." An ever-better financed and more militarized Immigration and Naturalization Service (INS) deported more than a million Latinos a year. Responding to pressures brought by Latinos and human rights activists, police departments in New York, Chicago, Santa Ana, San Jose, and other cities agreed not to cooperate with the INS.

Many Americans scapegoated Latino immigrants for "taking our jobs," even though few Americans wanted the underpaid jobs that immigrants accepted.[7] As political scientist Harry Pachon told a reporter: "They are not talking about middle-class Asian engineers, but day laborers and gardeners [who] . . . are not competing for aerospace jobs. When Hughes and Lockheed move away, those were not undocumented workers. We are looking for scapegoats."[8] In fact, the influx of immigrants helped revitalize dying industries in cities like Miami and Los Angeles. The *Wall Street Journal* reported that immigrants provided "the margin of survival for entire sectors" and were the "backbone" of the economy in some states.[9]

Latino immigrants were also accused of being responsible for tax increases needed to fund bilingual school classes and social welfare programs. Actually, a four-billion-dollar government program of assistance to the states helped defray these costs. In 1971 the Supreme Court had ruled that "resident aliens" must have equal access to state welfare programs. But less than 6 percent of Latino immigrants today are on welfare, collect unemployment checks, or use food stamps. Those who lack documents proving their legal right to be here are ineligible for most welfare programs. Yet their paycheck deductions help beef up welfare funds for the rest of the population. Tens of billions of dollars in salary contributions by "undocumented" immigrant workers have kept the sinking Social Security trust fund afloat for years ("undocumented" immigrants rarely collected Social Security).

Prominent members of both political parties proposed draconian measures against the "undocumented." President Clinton's proposed health care plan ruled out any coverage for them. Republican Governor Pete Wilson of California called for a constitutional amendment to deny citizenship to their U.S.-born children.[10]

The harassment of Latinos suspected of being "illegals" escalated to bizarre levels. For example, conservative light-skinned Linda Chavez, the former head of the U.S. Civil Rights Commission under President Reagan, was detained at the U.S.-Canadian border because the Border Patrol did not accept her driver's license as proof of citizenship. Herself an early critic of "undocumented immigrants," Chavez later sided with pro-immigrant groups by calling for higher levels of legal immigration and bilingual education. She rejected proposals that would require all U.S. citizens and legal residents to carry national identity cards. Other critics of the identification cards have compared them to the "pass" cards historically used in South Africa's apartheid system to segregate blacks.

Employers were glad about the arrival of the new Latino immigrants, anxious to take advantage of their hard work at substandard wages. Mexican immigrant workers told this writer in 1981 of how "The employers tell us,

'Come, don't stop coming, you are the ones who get the job done—if you don't come, we'll lose everything.'"[11] Of course, when some of the "undocumented" immigrants began forming unions and winning court decisions protecting their rights, the same employers backed a new immigration law—the 1986 Immigration Reform and Control Act (IRCA)—that made the unions illegal by stripping the "undocumented" of all their rights.[12]

The majority of the new Latino immigrants were Mexican, but by 1995 there were more than two million Central Americans fleeing civil wars. Cubans and Dominicans numbered a million each. South Americans numbered nearly two million, some of whom, like so many of the Central Americans, had escaped U.S.-backed military regimes and "death squads."[13]

Not all of the immigrants were treated equally. The largest group of Cubans arrived in the years right after the Cuban Revolution of 1959. They were from the lighter-skinned, better-educated, wealthy sectors of the Cuban population who disliked the revolution's reforms. The U.S. government, opposing the Cuban Revolution, welcomed them. Congress passed the Cuban Refugee Program, providing a billion dollars to help them find jobs and housing. The nation's first bilingual programs in public schools were created for them. Many Puerto Ricans and other Latinos wondered what they had to do to gain equally favorable treatment.[14]

In 1980 some poorer Cubans arrived. Because they launched their boats from the Cuban port of Mariel, they were called "Marielitos." They too were eligible for political refugee status and federal assistance, although some turned out to be criminals and mental patients and were returned to Cuba. In the 1990s, as aid from the former Soviet Union stopped arriving and the U.S. economic embargo against Cuba tightened, more Cubans came to the United States to share in the special programs for Cubans. In 1994 President Clinton decided to turn back Cuban "boat" or "raft" people, housing them in barbed-wired camps in a complex policy seeking to please anti-immigrant Americans and to further undermine the revolutionary regime in Cuba, with an eye to winning the votes of thousands of Cuban exiles who hoped to "liberate" Cuba.

People fleeing U.S.-supported dictatorships or civil wars in Latin America were not given the welcome granted to the Cubans from 1959 to 1994 or, in the 1980s, to the Nicaraguans opposed to their country's 1979 revolution. Some Dominicans were unofficial political refugees fleeing a dictatorship set up by U.S. Marines in 1965 to prevent the restoration to power of a president toppled by the Dominican Army. Other Dominicans were "boat people"—desperate refugees fleeing poverty by boarding wooden vessels to cross the shark-ridden waters of the Mona Passage to Puerto Rico. Low-paid young women from the Dominican Republic, Colombia, and other lands were increasingly recruited by New York's garment industry to replace unionized Puerto Ricans.[15]

Many immigrants were dark-skinned political refugees from Central America or Haiti, but they were not granted refugee status. Thousands of Salvadorans, Guatemalans, and Haitians, including some schoolchildren, were herded into barbed-wire holding pens described by journalists as "concentration camps."[16] Every major human rights group condemned the government's inhumane policies. A 100,000-strong "sanctuary movement" of mostly church people sheltered Central American refugees in defiance of the immigration laws.[17]

In some places, Latino immigrant children registered in schools with no questions asked about legal status. In others, like Texas, schools often turned them away. Not until 1982 in *Plyler v. Doe* did the Supreme Court decide that the "equal protection" clause of the Fourteenth Amendment meant that children of "illegal" immigrant workers had to be allowed into public schools. There they were often "pushed out" by humiliating treatment. One

Latina immigrant who dropped out of school later recalled: "You couldn't say *one word* in Spanish. You would get expelled or get a whipping."[18] Many children of immigrant workers were put to work in violation of child labor laws, amended in 1977 to lower the cutoff age to twelve. They missed school classes at harvest time.

As they had always done, earlier Latino immigrants sought to assist newly arriving ones. Starting in the late 1970s, for example, Ecuadorians, Dominicans, and others at New York City's nonprofit Universidad de los Trabajadors (Workers University) helped many newcomers learn English, find jobs, and prepare for the GED or college entrance exams.[19]

The education of immigrant children remains a major problem. Today, more than twenty million residents are foreign-born. Special language programs are needed, but more than 80 percent of the nation's schoolteachers are white and untrained in multicultural sensitivity or foreign languages. A white backlash against dark-skinned immigrants is targeting Latino schoolchildren, as illustrated by California's 1994 election campaign.

California's Governor Wilson advocated barring the children of "illegal" immigrants from attending school, but under the 1982 Supreme Court ruling that remained illegal. In the 1994 campaign, Wilson found himself trailing in the polls by more than twenty points because of voter discontent with the state's failing economy, hard hit by the end of the Cold War and U.S. defense budget cutbacks. By scapegoating immigrants for the state's economic problems and by backing an anti-immigrant referendum measure known as "Proposition 187," Wilson recovered his popularity in the polls and handily won reelection.

Proposition 187 passed by a three-to-two margin. It barred from the state's public schools any person unable to prove his or her U.S. citizenship. It prohibited any "illegal immigrant" from attending the state's community college and university system. It also denied "illegal immigrants" public health services (except for emergency care) and welfare benefits (already denied them in most instances). A "snitch" clause in Proposition 187 required all state offices and personnel to report "suspected" illegal immigrants and their parents or guardians to the police or the INS, opening the doors to a witchhunt. Many teachers angrily refused to "police" their students, most of whom were U.S.-born (but not necessarily to U.S. citizen parents). California's Latinos, Asians, and other minorities mobilized massive demonstrations of 70,000 or more to protest 187's frontal assault on basic human and constitutional rights. Chicano and other Latino students and teachers stormed out of school classrooms in 1960s-style "blowouts." Judges issued restraint orders prohibiting the enforcement of Proposition 187. Even 187's supporters acknowledged that its contents were unconstitutional.

Latinos trying to educate their children have to put up with this kind of backlash at every turn. They face repeated discrimination fueled by lies and half-truths infusing the rising tide of immigrant bashing. For example, Latinos are frequently called "irresponsible" and "unpatriotic." But opinion surveys have shown that most Latinos believe in individual responsibility and in helping others. Since many have had firsthand experiences with dictatorships, they are every bit as "patriotic" in the commitment to democracy and its values as any other American, sometimes more so. Puerto Ricans and Mexicans are often said to be "culturally deficient." The public ranked them at the bottom, just above gypsies, in a 1989 National Opinion Research Center survey ranking thirty-seven racial and ethnic categories in "social standing."[20]

All these criticisms filter down to the children, undermining their self-confidence and their chances to succeed at school. It becomes very difficult to "Americanize" when so many Americans think of you as the darker-skinned "other." Light-skinned Europeans didn't have that problem.

Latinos take advantage of bilingual programs wherever they can find them and learn English quickly. As one writer on immigrants told the *New York Times*: "It is the parents' language, not English, that is endangered."[21] Far from intending to replace English with Spanish, bilingual programs in the schools aim to assist persons for whom English is difficult or "a second language." Today, the government mandates bilingual instruction for grades where at least twenty students are "Limited English Proficient" (LEP) and have the same native language. If the number is smaller, then ESL (English as a Second Language) services must be offered. ESL programs normally consist of small, flexible classes, using simple words, visual aids, and gestures to teach vocabulary.

Experts may differ on the specifics but they agree on a few basic ingredients for a successful bilingual program. Teachers should know the languages of the students involved. Rather than drills or lesson plans, they should emphasize group learning with lots of reading, talking, and writing—always using and developing each student's first language. Recent studies show that Latinos whose first language is Spanish do best in acquiring English proficiency if their classes are taught in Spanish before switching over to English. These students are more likely to achieve a normal rate of academic progress. In fact, the most successful Latino high-school students are the ones most proficient in both Spanish and English.[22] The College Board reports that students who take foreign languages for five years score better on SATs than those with little or no second-language instruction.[23]

Most bilingual programs emphasize the "transition to English approach" and learning about the dominant culture ("Americanization"). Unfortunately, some critics say, the programs tend to segregate the learners and to reinforce "society's power relations."[24]

Just as many schools ignored the *Brown* decision and continued their segregationist policies, a majority of the nation's schools have defied the federal mandate for bilingual

Students in a bilingual class show off their history textbooks.

education. Consequently, most Latinos not fluent in English are attending mainstream classes without understanding much of the instruction being offered them. On the other hand, those segregated into language-training classes suffer the negative consequences of isolation. Either way, the *Brown* and *Lau* decisions concerning equality in educational opportunity are violated.

Some educators believe that only "two-way" bilingual classrooms can overcome the dilemma. "Two-way" bilingual education has, in fact, had some notable success. Often both the English-speaking and the Spanish-speaking children learning "side by side . . . assisting each other" have become "fluent bilinguals while making good progress in other subjects."[25] At a school in a small city of New York's Hudson River Valley, a teacher informed a visitor to her classes:

> *My first graders are all English-speaking, Ana's are Spanish-speaking. We each teach academic subjects to our own classes in their own language. I teach English to her class every day. She teaches Spanish to mine. We mix them for art, music, gym, library and lunch. They understand each other and pick up books in both languages. It's enriching for both groups.*[26]

As educational costs rose and with them taxes, opponents of bilingual programs launched major campaigns against them. This had a chilling effect on "the Lau Remedies" put forward by the U.S. Commission of Education and the Office of Civil Rights in 1975. The Lau Remedies, based on the famous 1974 Supreme Court *Lau* decision mandating bilingual education, provided for the teaching of courses like math and science in the student's native language while learning English-language skills. Educators wondered what the curtailment of the Lau Remedies meant for the growing number of LEP children, whose numbers were expected to triple to six million by the turn of the century.

An "Americanization" campaign in education reminiscent of earlier times has emphasized learning English and the usefulness of ESL instruction as a quick fix, "transitional" approach. It has even paid lip service to "cultural diversity" and "multiculturalism." Yet it has also included controversial calls to make English the nation's "official language."[27]

In the 1980s and 1990s, a group of racial bigots and genuinely concerned citizens joined an organization calling itself "U.S. English." It launched a well-financed "English only" movement that succeeded in making English the "official language" in more than a dozen states, including heavily Latino ones like California, Arizona, Colorado, and Florida. It posed as a "liberal-minded" nonprofit educational organization that is still classified as a tax-exempt "charity" by the Internal Revenue Service. By presenting a liberal veneer of protecting children's rights to learn English, it was better able to attack any form of bilingual education beyond the bare "transitional" minimum typical of most bilingual programs. The Reagan administration pushed the 1988 Bilingual Education Act through Congress, limiting the length of bilingual education for a student to three years maximum.[28]

When the New York State Board of Regents proposed to keep LEP children a little longer in bilingual classrooms, U.S. English placed a full-page ad in the *New York Times* saying that children would be receiving "very limited instruction in English" and would "be denied the opportunity to participate fully in the American dream." The Board of Regents went ahead with its plan anyway, on the grounds that "research over the past two decades . . . lends strong support for developing students' native language and literacy skills while they learn English."[29] Most of the nation's existing bilingual programs were already too abbreviated and too "transitional" to allow students a realistic chance at academic success.

Supporters of U.S. English believe that the best way to learn English is through placing a student with English-language speakers as soon as possible (sometimes called "deep immersion"). Evidence shows that learning is far more complicated. While it is true that children whose first language is Spanish or Vietnamese often learn simple English phrases and chatter with their classmates during recess, it is also true that they learn how to read and write and develop abstract reasoning skills better when they are taught in their native tongue. Once literate and comfortable in basic skills in their own language, it is easier for them to switch to English. Research studies have confirmed that if children are forced to make the switch too early, they succeed in neither language.[30]

In the words of James Crawford, Washington editor of *Education Week*:

> *there are no shortcuts to English proficiency. . . . A fixation on teaching English as quickly as possible fails to prepare students to compete on equal terms. When their first language is cultivated along with English, students are equipped to develop normally. They enter the mainstream later, but with improved chances of success and with the added dividend of fluency in two languages. . . . [Moreover] adults and adolescents acquire languages more efficiently than children.*[31]

Then why does U.S. English so strongly combat the spread of bilingualism in the schools? Raúl Yzaguirre, president of the National Council of La Raza, gives us a significant clue: "U.S. English," he says, "is to Hispanics as the Ku Klux Klan is to blacks." In other words, U.S. English is a deeply political, nativist, and anti-Latino group. On national television, First Lady Barbara Bush characterized U.S. English's proposed amendment to the U.S. Constitution to make English the official language as "a racial slur."[32]

The "Founding Fathers," after all, rejected the idea as blatantly unfair.[33] The Articles of Confederation were written in English, French, and German. The eighteenth and nineteenth centuries were marked by multilingualism, and German-language schooling continued into the twentieth. Warns one educator about the "English only" movement: "Tyrannies of the majority are ultimately self- defeating. . . . [so-called] 'American' identity cannot be propagated, nor ethnic harmony assured, by means that contradict our [nation's] founding principles."[34] Two other educators point out: "If there is to be democracy in the 21st century, it must be multiracial/multicultural democracy."[35]

It also helps to know something about the leadership and funding of U.S. English. It was founded by U.S. Senator S. I. Hayakawa, a Democrat from Hawaii who died in 1992, and Dr. John Tanton, an environmentalist and population control advocate from Michigan. In 1979, Tanton had launched the right-wing lobbying group FAIR (Federation for American Immigration Reform). U.S. English hired former Reagan official Linda Chavez as its president after her failed Senate campaign of 1986.

Chavez soon found out that Tanton personally had accepted the endorsement of five known Nazi groups, as well as funding from the white supremacist Pioneer Fund, dedicated to "race betterment" through eugenics. By means of a poll of regular contributors to U.S. English, Chavez discovered that 42 percent of them believed the United States should "stand strong and not cave in to Hispanics who shouldn't be here."[36]

Resigning from U.S. English in disgust, Chavez warned people against the organization's racism and debunked the idea of returning to the old days when children were forced "to sink or swim in classes in which they don't understand the language of instruction."[37] By speaking out for the bilingual programs U.S. English had denounced, she sided with major civil rights organizations like LULAC and MALDEF that had founded the one-year-old English Plus Information Clearinghouse (EPIC).[38]

EPIC called for "cultural and democratic pluralism" and the fostering of "multiple language skills." Its approach was tried in the economically depressed area of Lowell, Massachusetts. Latinos united with Cambodian refugees and other Asians to obtain "English plus" bilingual programs in the public schools, where they composed 40 percent of the students. In 1987 a white backlash in Lowell won an "English only" referendum. Critics called it "the bigot bill." Said one, a descendant of Italians and French Canadians: "If bilingual education works, why throw it out just because your ancestors didn't have it? Child labor also existed for immigrant families in the 1890s. Should we return to those days, or should we progress as a society?"[39]

Ironically, in California, a state where one-fourth of the residents are Latino, voters also approved an "English as the Official Language" initiative. Latinos fought back against the new nativist movement and won several court victories declaring "English only" statutes unconstitutional.[40] Few states bothered enforcing the impractical local laws in the schools anyway. In fact, California joined New York and other states in offering the GED examinations for high-school equivalency diplomas in Spanish. A major problem today, reports *Hispanic* magazine, is "a shortage of about 175,000 bilingual teachers."[41] This is the largest shortage in any field of education. Moreover, teachers are not being trained fast enough to keep up with the need.

Not enough bilingual Latinos enter teachers colleges and train for these important jobs. In the 1950s, all students had to learn a second language to graduate from high school. This requirement ended, and a 1979 Presidential commission stated that "Americans' gross inadequacy in foreign-language skills is nothing short of scandalous."[42] Now government officials, business executives, and educators are championing mastery of more than one language to deal with the realities of today's "global economy" and our racially tense, culturally diverse society. As one commentator on "transitional" bilingual programs notes: "If there is any injustice in bilingual education in the United States, it is that children who speak the majority or dominant language are not often exposed to education in two languages."[43]

Some Latinos say that none of the bilingual programs will work without a multicultural approach that encourages non-English speaking children instead of segregating or stigmatizing them. But, they say, a multicultural approach must do more than merely celebrate "mariachis, tacos, and fiestas" and install cultural pride. They call for a more challenging and truthful education about the nation's cultural diversity, including differences within each group and sub-group (for example, differences between Chicanos in northern New Mexico and Chicanos in East Los Angeles). They say we must educate every student about all cultures.

They oppose linguistic, gender, racial, or physical segregation or discrimination in educational institutions. Recognizing the need for fluency and literacy in English, to achieve it they recommend bilingual-multicultural programs that help all students understand more than one language, as well as the differences in languages, value systems, and histories among different groups of people. They propose "mixing" students of different racial or cultural backgrounds so that they can learn from one another.

Otherwise, they fear that bilingual programs will end up being another form of "Americanization." As one Latino critic puts it, the programs will "mold" the child "into an acceptable English-speaking American."[44] Adds another: "Most Puerto Rican educators agree that Puerto Rican pupils need not only [bilingual education] . . . but also . . . what is actually taught in the schools needs to be tied to the student's life experiences."[45]

Despite all the obstacles and criticisms, a number of bilingual programs have done remarkably well. A group of researchers from different backgrounds investigated a "mixed" elementary school in central California attended by mostly Mexican immigrants and Chicanos. Responding to strong community pressures and using some good old-fashioned common sense, the school introduced "IBT" teacher teams—Immersion/Bilingual Teams, with the immersion in Spanish instead of English. The researchers found that everyone benefited. The school was transformed "from a white, Anglo institution that disenfranchises ethnic children to an institution that values and celebrates ethnic diversity as a source of motivation to succeed."[46]

P.S. 84, an elementary school in New York City's borough of Manhattan, introduced a similar approach where students alternated daily between a Spanish classroom and an English classroom. Team-teaching was used. Milwaukee's Fratney Street School (La Escuela Fratney) developed the bilingual, multicultural model further when the community saved the old school building from destruction. Its innovative approaches improved race relations and discouraged sexist practices. Chicago's Roberto Clemente High School, an extended "community school" keeping its doors open in the evening for recreational activities, health services, drug counseling, training programs, and teaching literacy classes to adults, also used bilingual, multicultural approaches effectively. San Antonio's Partners for Valued Youth program of instructional cross-age tutoring for LEP middle-school children reduced the dropout rate and increased test scores.[47]

There have been many experiments like these, but most succeed only because their teachers, staff, children, and parents work extra hard. Without nationwide or even statewide or citywide backing, they are a bit like throwing a glass of water on a forest fire. Nonetheless, it is now at last widely recognized that a broader and improved implementation of bilingualism is necessary if educational equity is ever to be achieved.

8

ocho

"ONE NATION, MANY PEOPLES"

The public school [is] . . . an educator for the educated rich and a keeper for the uneducated poor. There exists no more powerful force of social class and the frustration of natural potential.

—John Coons, 1970[1]

Countless government reports agree on one thing: our schools, not our children, are flunking.[2] Television specials, radio talk shows, and best sellers like Jonathan Kozol's *Savage Inequalities* brand our public schools "the shame of the nation." One commentator summarizes the findings of a wide array of experts:

> *public schooling is rigged to favor middle-class students and to ensure that working-class students do poorly enough to convince them that they fully merit the lowly station that will one day be theirs. "Our goal is to get these kids to be like their parents," one teacher, more candid than most, remarked to a Carnegie researcher. . . . Vocational programs . . . notes Sizer . . . "are often a cruel social dumping ground."*[3]

To some, it seems as though no one realizes how completely the teaching of the three Rs (reading, writing, and arithmetic) are taking a backseat to the three Cs—common culture, conformity, and command of English.[4] Many favor a return to "the basics"—a more up-to-date name for the three Rs. In *A Nation at Risk,* the National Commission on Excellence in Education warns against a "rising tide of mediocrity." Today, more than half the nation's children test out as "at risk."

Citing *A Nation at Risk* and similar reports, the Bush administration issued a call to arms endorsed by the Clinton administration as well: "Goals 2000: Educate America." Under the plan, by the year 2000 "all children in America" will start out "ready to learn" in "safe, disciplined, and drug-free" schools. They will achieve competency in "core" subjects, including science, where the nation will move from near the bottom among industrialized countries to "first in the world." Students will attain a 90 percent high school graduation rate. Finally, all adults will be literate and "possess the skills necessary to compete in a global economy."

Most Americans polled by public opinion surveys

approve of the goals but are skeptical that they can be achieved. Many agree with education writer Walter Karp's assessment that "The education of a free people will not come from federal bureaucrats crying up 'excellence' for 'economic growth,' any more than it came from their predecessors who cried up schooling as a means to 'get a better job'."[5]

Other critics point out that although Goals 2000 is a federal plan, it is receiving very little government money and is being implemented largely through the creation of a few hundred model schools funded by profit-making private outfits like Education Alternatives, Inc. (EAI), the New American Schools Development Corporation, and the Edison Project of controversial advertising-publishing wizard Christopher Whittle. This attempted conversion of schools into profit centers is part of a trend to commercialize and privatize education. It usually favors families who can afford it, the already favored.[6]

When *Hispanic* magazine asked Secretary of Education Richard Riley about what Goals 2000 was doing for Hispanics, he gave an answer that could be interpreted as stereotyping Latinos. He said that the Clinton administration had added core competencies "that are very important to Hispanic Americans, that is, foreign languages . . . and also the arts."[7]

One of the strongest defenders of Goals 2000 is The Conference Board, a group of executives from large corporations. In reviewing a decade of efforts since *A Nation at Risk* was published, the Board concluded in 1993 that there was "not yet . . . documented wide-scale improvement."[8]

So far, "back to basics" favors middle-class youngsters and slights those most in need. The $6.1 billion "Chapter 1" program, the federal government's main avenue for improving the basic skills of the poor, still excludes LEP (Limited English Proficient) students and the children of migrant workers. New York State's allocation from federal Emergency Immigrant Education Assistance funds was cut by half in 1991–92 from its already reduced 1990 level at a time when the number of new immigrants in the state was tripling. Counting both children and adults, there are sixty to eighty million children and adults in need of basic skills. Few among them are receiving any attention, and those who do are usually the least needy.

A commonly heard complaint by students and teachers of all income groups is that "back to basics" programs sometimes deter genuine learning. Youngsters actually learn and understand very little in chemistry or other core subjects because teachers "stop being experimental and innovative and 'teach to the test'."[9] This is because standardized testing has become more widespread than ever before in an effort to make schools more efficient and "accountable" for teaching the "basics."

More than one team of Latino educators has criticized the "accountability movement" for its fixation on testing—a mentality of "if it moves, test it!"[10] Even the president of the Council for Basic Education acknowledges that "testing does not guarantee students will be competent in basic skills, because many important basic skills are not measured and many others . . . [such as] critical thinking and the ability to write . . . are unmeasurable, given the state of the art in testing."[11] Although profitable for the companies, textbook producers, and personnel involved in the curriculum/testing business, the "testing on basics" approach is proving more effective in tracking students than in educating them.

Most educators now recognize that tracking is unfair, even to many "advanced" students. According to the president of the National Action Council for Minorities in Engineering, a "vast body of research clearly shows that tracking systems by any of their names—magnet schools, gifted and talented programs, theme schools—benefit no one, except perhaps teachers, who have an easier time working with homogeneous groups."[12]

Yet the practice of "ability grouping," often based on standardized testing, continues with devastating results for today's children. Teachers are complaining that when they look at lower tracks they see "increasing numbers of emotionally and physically damaged children suffering from poverty, crime and drugs," while the higher tracks of "'advantaged' children often [are] lacking curiosity, kindness, compassion, and joy."[13] Mixed-ability groups, on the other hand, often generate less selfish and better-educated students who also achieve higher test scores. Partly this is because the mixed groups are in schools that are making an extra special effort to end tracking and upgrade school performance.[14]

In 1989 a preliminary report by a task force on minorities for the New York State Commissioner of Education shocked the nation. It criticized the schools' "Eurocentric" curriculum, saying it contained "hidden assumptions of white supremacy."[15] That same year, the so-called Bradley Commission, composed of leading U.S. historians, issued a book-length report on how to build a history curriculum.[16] The report called for a more multicultural education. It attacked standardized testing and multiple choice questions as detrimental to an historical perspective and critical thinking—a view now widely accepted. SAT preparers are already beginning to reduce the number of multiple-choice questions.

In 1991 New York State's Board of Regents approved a more complete report than that of the 1989 task force. Entitled *One Nation, Many Peoples: A Declaration of Cultural Interdependence*, the new report recognized the nation's "current reality . . . [of] racial and ethnic pluralism" and the many "virtues of diversity." It recommended a curricular overhaul to provide a multicultural, anti-racist and anti-sexist education. The Regents mandated that these recommendations be carried out. A series of committees of experts proceeded to start drafting a new multicultural curriculum for grades kindergarten-to-twelve to take effect in the late 1990s. The committees encouraged local school autonomy and choice of readings.[17]

Practical necessities, and not just earlier empowerment movements, had set New York and other large states along this new path. Small but startling first steps are now being taken to modify the dominant "Americanization" (WASP, Eurocentric) approach to education, especially in the social sciences and humanities—social studies, history, literature, and the arts.

Initiated in California in 1987, the new multicultural initiative is still in its infancy. It seeks to incorporate some long-omitted information about "everyday people"—a curriculum of inclusion, not exclusion. By teaching a more complete history, introducing multiple perspectives, and expanding young people's horizons, multiculturalism aims to ameliorate racism, anti-Semitism, and other pernicious forms of hatred and to create more literate citizens capable of critical thinking.

Yet even something as carefully prepared and monitored as this modest educational reform has evoked an outcry of passionate controversy. Demagogic academicians have gained headlines with inflammatory statements damning some "other" group. Commentators on New York City's local ABC television news have gone so far as to allege that multiculturalism will generate an apartheid-type school system—apparently unaware that one already exists in most parts of the country, especially New York.

Sadly, the 1992 acquittal of four Los Angeles policemen accused of excessive use of force in the arrest of speeding black motorist Rodney King provided fresh urgency and justification for multicultural education. The jury's verdict defied what people saw in their living rooms on the frequently played videotapes of the beating. Not one African American sat on the jury. The verdict represented a classic case of negative stereotyping, or what sociologists call "selective perception." The jurors saw what they had been conditioned to see, what they wanted to believe. In the riot-rebellion that followed the verdict, half the residents in the hardest hit neighborhoods of Los Angeles were Latino, as were half of those arrested.[18]

After the flames of South Central Los Angeles died down, polls showed an anxious public asking why the government was not doing more to help the have-nots. "Their" problems affected "us." Solutions had to be found! "Don't just talk—do something about it!" became a common refrain. The question of how to revise public education assumed fresh urgency. The issue of how to use our schools as a learning ground for alleviating racism and improving economic opportunity has placed multicultural education smack in the center of the national agenda.

In the early 1990s, George Bush, the self-proclaimed "Education President," liked to cite the high success rates of the Head Start program and the handful of schools experimenting with enrichment programs—so-called "magnet" schools created to attract the brightest students of all races. But most people realize these programs are not nearly enough. Head Start programs are not widely available, while the magnet schools are, as noted by education writer Jonathan Kozol, "disproportionately white and middle class" because they are based on entry tests and teachers' recommendations.[19]

To fill the urgent need, a much reported school reform movement has emerged, experimenting with several ideas. Most efforts emphasize increased local autonomy ("community control") and marketplace solutions of "choice." Unfortunately, "choice" usually turns out to be "choice for the chosen." *Rethinking Schools* editor Bob Peterson opposes "marketplace solutions of choice" because "they have done such a miserable job of solving problems of housing, jobs and health care."[20]

The tuition tax credit movement or "voucher plan" is the best known "choice" alternative. It is strongly backed by "born again" Christians and the New Right (85 percent of private school enrollments are in church-affiliated schools).

This "choice" encourages the privatization of education by granting tax reductions as partial reimbursement of tuition costs paid by parents who send their children to private schools. Lawyers and judges doubt its constitutionality on many grounds, including those of separation of church and state and equal protection of the laws. *Hispanic* magazine has warned that the voucher plan would likely "result in even greater budget cuts for public schools."[21] Several states have conducted referendums on the voucher plan. In 1993 voters in California rejected it for a third time—by a margin of seven-to-three.

Some states, including California, Florida, and Oklahoma, have introduced a variant of the "schools as profit centers" approach. In the name of "self-help," they have created education foundation consortiums. However, these private groups have raised very little money, and incidents of theft and fraud have tarnished their record.[22]

"Special education" classes, attended largely by blacks and Latinos, are growing by leaps and bounds. Few students who enroll in them go on to graduate, however. Youngsters assigned from an early age to special education classes feel ostracized and hopeless. Remedial instruction is stigmatized instead of rewarded. Schools that "mainstream" instead of "ghettoize" remedial students by integrating them in more regular school classes do better. Pupils can still be pulled out of a regular classroom one hour a day to receive special instruction.[23]

Numerous community-based schools, including some of those described in the previous chapter, have successfully implemented the "mainstreaming" and "mixed setting" approach. They emphasize "participatory and interactive learning." They use oral history and encourage pupils to work on projects together, sometimes even producing small pamphlets or books.[24]

In a new approach to "mixture" and desegregation, some school districts are beginning to experiment with assigning elementary school students on the basis of income.

Poor students and affluent ones are "mixed" in a single school.[25]

A graduation requirement at a growing number of secondary schools is some form of community service, often in elementary schools. This becomes another way of "mixing" students, both by race and age, when older students help younger ones needing assistance in the lower grades.

So-called "charter" schools involving teachers, parents, and community are becoming common. While some border on being "schools for profit," many are committed to the public school system and upgrading education for the poor. Philadelphia has several of these schools, some of them nicknamed "Comer schools" after the career-development and "service skills" ideas of Dr. James Comer, director of the School Development Program at Yale's Child Study Center.[26]

Funding for all the new programs has concerned many people. In 1994 voters in Michigan approved a proposition shifting school financing from reliance on property taxes to higher state sales and cigarette taxes. This shifts much of the burden of public school funding from home-owning taxpayers to those who can't even afford a home. It also fails to tackle the question of what kind of education children receive.

Regardless of how much money is involved, educational experts agree that no school reforms will ever help out the majority of young people unless educational funding is made more *equal*. Some suggest that all school districts be budgeted equally from a common federal tax fund. Others recommend radically raising poor neighborhoods' tax bases by providing decent good-paying employment for all. Less direct ways have also been suggested.[27]

Almost every school success story depends on a group of hardworking teachers and students who have the support of school principals or the community. Funding has not proven to be the key ingredient, although better-funded schools still tend to produce higher achievers.

The 1988 hit movie *Stand and Deliver,* starring Edward James Olmos and based on a true story, carries to its logical extreme the message of "work harder and you will succeed." A Chicano teacher (Olmos) works so many extra hours to improve the calculus test scores of his Chicano students that he suffers a heart attack. When the students do exceptionally well on their calculus SATs, the testing board assumes they cheated. They take the tests again and this time the board accepts their high scores. The film's obvious message is that racism is overbearing but if you try hard enough you can still "make it." Its hidden message is: "If they can make it, why can't you?" Unfortunately, most youngsters who watch the film do not have such self-sacrificing teachers.

No single proposed set of reforms seems to be as pivotal or as complete as multiculturalism. Most branches of the school reform movement pay at least lip service to it, although many citizens are still confused about what multiculturalism means. Many white people have a stereotyped view of it as a thinly veiled African-American threat against "our" European traditions. This attitude reflects the very kind of "*they* are coming to get *us*" view of reality that multiculturalism seeks to eradicate.

Funding and staffing for implementing multicultural programs remains sparse. Although some public schools are beginning to introduce them, few teachers are able to handle the challenge. As of 1992 there were hardly any courses at all on cultural diversity in the nation's teacher training programs.[28] Besides calling for a required multicultural curriculum at all teachers' colleges, some educators have suggested offering future teachers who want to work in inner-city schools higher wages after completing a two-year in-depth training program.

At the college level, the record is also spotty. Only 54 percent of public four-year colleges and 23 percent of two-year ones had a required multicultural course in 1992. Usually, the multicultural requirement was so minimal and tokenistic that campus wits sarcastically nicknamed it "multicultural tourism" or "the cafeteria approach." Civil rights movement veteran Elizabeth Martinez has bitterly described the typical multiculturalism requirement as having students "take a main dish of Black beings here, a little Latino spice there, some inscrutable-Oriental salad over yonder, and a Native American ceremony for dessert."[29]

Feelings of frustration have led some multiculturalism advocates to adopt narrowly nationalistic positions that are easy to ridicule. Mainstream conservative radio and television personalities like Rush Limbaugh are having a field day taking pot shots at them. Martinez has lamented that "people of color" who want to build "new [multiracial, multiethnic] coalitions" find themselves "compelled to focus on white supremacist assaults upon multiculturalism." The result is often a reinvigorated "push toward separatism and anger at whiteness" at a time when "we need, urgently need, such [new] coalitions."[30]

Critics of multiculturalism ask questions like: "Will Shakespeare and Dickens be thrown out and replaced by Langston Hughes [an African-American writer] and Anzia Yezierska [a Jewish-American writer]?" "Will all the good things about European culture be slighted and our identity as Americans be lost?" "Will African Americans get most of the attention while other groups receive correspondingly less?" These questions confirm historian Ronald Takaki's assessment that what is fueling the debate over "the content of our curriculum is America's intensifying racial crisis."[31]

The answer to all of these questions is *no*. One's identity as an American will be enriched by an appreciation of who Americans are in all their diversity. For reasons of time and practicality, youngsters will, of course, read less Shakespeare, but they will also become familiar with a far wider range of literature.

Still, the doubters ask, "Shouldn't families and not the schools teach their children about their own ethnic and racial heritage?" This is the position of teacher-union leader and syndicated columnist Albert Shanker. It ignores the reality of many children having two working parents or a single parent, often unable to afford the time or the money for books and videotapes needed to learn at home. As importantly, it skirts the issue of children learning about other cultures and other peoples' perspectives, a necessary corrective for the lack of information that so often underlies racism. One junior-high-school teacher in a wealthy white suburban community, echoing Shanker's failure to recognize multiculturalism's value to whites, informed a visitor that his school did "not need multiculturalism because we don't have any blacks or Hispanics here, just one or two Asians."[32]

Some people, usually nonwhites, ask "Why should Jews who are largely middle class be included?" This too misses the point of multiculturalism—educating children about all groups, especially those disenfranchised, discriminated against, or otherwise oppressed and too often unmentioned in schoolbooks. It also ignores the true story of Jewish Americans and underestimates the stubborn persistence and impact of anti-Semitism and its deep interrelationship to racism here and overseas.[33]

Still others wonder if the multicultural agenda is not too political, perhaps even undemocratic. The truth is that all education is politically tinged, but not all education is democratic. Advocates of multicultural education say that multiculturalism represents a great advance in the endeavor to fulfill the American Dream of democracy. In New York State, for example, the nascent multicultural curriculum emphasizes and illuminates the democratic values underlying the building of the United States, but not at the expense of denying the nation's shortcomings.

The 1991 report *One Nation, Many Peoples,* used by New York State's Department of Education to help create a multicultural curriculum, insists that social studies courses should examine and understand six ideas relating to democracy and disenfranchised peoples. First, democracy is an ongoing process. Second, the applications of the Constitution and Bill of Rights are products of a concerted effort by many peoples. Third, the inalienable right of liberty must be constantly fought for and protected. Fourth, democracy's strength derives from the possibility of successful struggle on behalf of freedom. Fifth, the strengthening of democracy has come about "through the determined efforts of those who, suffering from marginalization, have battled to gain their rights." And lastly, "racism, which has marred U.S. society since its founding, has been a formidable obstacle standing in the way of making the democratic ideals of America a reality for all."[34]

Saying that multiculturalism is political is the same thing as saying it is about empowerment. And it is. All education is about empowerment. As the old saying goes, "knowledge is power." What's different about multiculturalism is that it offers an education of inclusion instead of exclusion. It aims to empower everyone—the foundation of democracy.

What does a typical successful multicultural classroom look like?[35] Students actively participate in learning, instead of passively memorizing facts in the seventy-five-year-old tradition of "skill-and-drill." Educator John I. Goodlad reported in 1984 that less than 1 percent of classroom time in public schools consisted of student response with some kind of reasoned opinion.[36] Students often discover their own roots and the roots of others by interviewing family relatives and fellow students, reading short informative books with pictures, and keeping journals. All are encouraged to learn in an exciting way that interrelates knowledge from different subjects instead of atomizing a subject into a string of easily forgotten dates and names. Fast learners help slow ones, and sometimes older students and parents help younger ones. Unlike the majority of Americans, students in a multicultural classroom would be able to locate on a map such world "hot spots" as Korea, Somalia, Haiti, or Nicaragua.

To appreciate the many perspectives that exist on controversial issues, students use multiple learning techniques—role-playing, group activities, field trips, videotapes. After a few years of this approach, and often right from the start, students' test scores rise.

Instead of individualized guidance counseling that serves to produce hopelessness or perpetuates career or job tracking according to economic status, race, or gender, students attend a regular class in careers and jobs. Youngsters learn about a wide range of jobs through field trips, films, student research and oral reports, and guest appearances by workers and professionals, often parents from the community. Classes that identify the problems of stereotyping and racism/sexism are also an ongoing part of the curriculum. Moreover, they tie in with classes on history, literature, and careers, so that open and informed discussions occur on social problems of the day. English essay assignments deal with problems like AIDS, drug addiction, racism, sexism, or great events, instead of "how I spent my summer." Youngsters are educated to think about others instead of just themselves. They learn how to read newspapers or watch television critically, instead of automatically accepting whatever they read or hear. In other words, they learn how to think for themselves.

The media could contribute substantially to the new programs. On television, advertisers could devote their creative energies to imaginative ads, not just against drugs but against racism and sexism as well. The inadequate hour or two a week of educational programs offered by most stations could be increased and improved.

Naturally, if multiculturalism is to work on more than its present partial (some would say "tokenistic") basis, an ongoing national, state, and local consultation and evaluation will have to be maintained, not just by "experts," but by everyday people, especially parents and teachers. A number of educators believe that short of every student mastering a sequence of courses on something like "how to end racism and sexism forever," even the best-financed multi-cultural curriculum may fall short.

Many critics say that multicultural studies, however well intentioned, are simply too little and too late to address the urgent needs of the nation. Economic causes of bigotry and educational failure have to be addressed if multicultural education is to work, they insist. An unprecedented nationwide commitment may be necessary if we are to overcome what the U.S. Labor and Commerce Departments have called the trend toward a society of haves and have-nots and a breakdown of democracy (see Introduction and Chapter 6).

Rethinking Schools editor Peterson has sketched a scenario that appeals to many:

> *We should demand a national school reconstruction fund to rebuild inner city schools, radically reduce class size, and to create a new teacher corp. Such new schools should become centerpieces in our ravaged neighborhoods. They should be open 16 hours a day and serve as community centers in the evenings and weekends. Such intergenerational, recreational, cultural centers could become lifelines in our community. Such a massive program would have the side benefit of increasing the number of jobs in our cities, and begin to put urban schools on par with suburban schools by providing libraries, arts rooms, music rooms, performance areas, and computer rooms to the children who need such facilities the most. In Milwaukee we estimate that such an endeavor would require $232 million worth of new schools and $63 million in salaries to new teachers. This is equivalent to 10 hours of spending for the U.S. military budget last year.* [37]

A good education that is not matched by the creation of jobs will only lead to more Los Angeles's. If the nation's economic problems are not solved, Latinos' hard-won civil rights will continue to be undermined by the forces of poverty and white backlash. Many whites also realize that their futures are dim without better jobs. As former New York City Schools Chancellor Joseph A. Fernandez and others have pointed out, a program to rebuild America and revitalize the sluggish economy the way the Marshall Plan did in Europe at the end of World War II may be necessary if educational reforms are to have any genuine chance to succeed. It would go very far, Fernandez says, toward "getting rid of the frustration our kids have."[38]

Fortunately, the prospects for world peace since the end of the Cold War make this possible. A reallocation of funds would make a "Rebuilding America" program work. Reduced defense spending can yield most of the monies required. According to *The New York Times*, the nation's leading conservative economists recognized in 1992 the need for at least fifty billion dollars in new federal outlays in public works and education to facilitate economic recovery.[39] That's fifty times the 1994 education package signed by President Clinton.

The Public seems ready for some drastic changes. According to a January 1992 poll taken by CNN and *USA Today*, 55 percent of all Americans say that "the economy needs a complete overhaul." An earlier Gallup Poll indicated that 58 percent of the public was "willing to pay more taxes to help raise the standard of education."[40] Unemployment can be reduced if people are put to work rebuilding the nation's deteriorating schools, apartment buildings, highways, and railroads.

During a transitional period, multicultural education could be getting off the ground in our schools at a modest cost. Monies previously used for outmoded curricula and books could be shifted into funding new curricula and teaching materials. Funding for training of new teachers and upgrading the training of present teachers could also come from budgets traditionally used for teacher education. Nutritional breakfasts and lunches could be offered at every Head Start and elementary school.

Where already approved, multicultural programs could go a long way toward confronting and eventually ameliorating interracial and interethnic tensions plaguing so many cities. The initial programs can help prepare the ground for the many more changes needed to generate a more prosperous and democratic nation. Many people realize that failure to address these problems now will only lead to more costly alternatives later.

Latinos are among those most aware of these urgent educational issues. They have accomplished much since the days of their "invisibility." Today they see a quality education as doubly necessary if their children are to have any chance in life. We can be certain that they will keep up their impressive struggle to improve the nation's crisis-ridden educational system.

SOURCE NOTES

INTRODUCTION

1. Jonathan Kozol, *Savage Inequalities: Children in America's Schools* (New York: Crown, 1991), p. 212.

2. Quoted in Clara E. Rodríguez, *Puerto Ricans Born in the U.S.A.* (Boston: Unwin Hyman, Inc., 1989), p. 139.

3. Quoted in Herbert Grossman, *Educating Hispanic Students* (Springfield: Charles C Thomas, 1984), p. 10.

4. The terms *African American(s)* and *black(s)* are used interchangeably in this book. Only occasionally, when the context makes it clear, do we use the term *American(s)* to refer to all the people of the United States of America, because originally the term referred to all of the Western Hemisphere encountered by Columbus and other Europeans. Latin Americans resent the historically ignorant and culturally biased attempt by the United States to reserve the words *America* and *American* for itself. This book uses *Indian(s)* and *Native American(s)* interchangeably, without losing sight of the fact that the first peoples inhabiting this land were *not* European.

5. The term *Hispanic* became official usage in the 1980 Census. It was introduced in the 1970s in an apparent effort to depoliticize Latinos' energetic empowerment movements. Few Latinos liked the term at the time. It connotes "Spanish" or "Spain," the country against which the ancestors of most Latinos fought for national independence. This book uses the word *white(s)* to refer to non-Latino whites (since some Latinos are white-skinned). Often, as evidenced in Supreme Court decisions like the one applying *Brown* to Latinos in 1973 (see Chapter 2), the word *Anglo(s)* is used to refer to all whites, even though most whites are not of English ancestry. The reason is that the dominant culture in the United States is the one brought over from England—the "WASP" (White Anglo Saxon Protestant) one. Throughout this book, context determines usage—for instance, *Chicanos* for *Mexican Americans* after the early 1960s, when the word *Chicano* became widely used for U.S. citizens of Mexican descent. *Chicano* traditionally referred to working-class types and was used by upper-

class individuals to put them down. Politically active Chicanos used the term proudly, the way *black* became preferable to *Negro*. For more, see Rodolfo Acuña, *Occupied America: A History of Chicanos* (New York: Harper & Row, third ed., 1988), pp. ix–xi, 139, 379–386; James D. Cockcroft, *Latinos in the Making of the United States* (New York: Franklin Watts, 1995), Chapter 4.

6. Quoted in *New York Times*, June 3, 1994.

7. See James D. Cockcroft, *The Hispanic Struggle for Social Justice* (New York: Franklin Watts, 1994) and *Latinos in the Making*, and Hedda Garza, *Latinas: Hispanic Women in the United States* (New York: Franklin Watts, 1994).

8. Civil rights laws and educators use the word *minority* to refer to groups of people with less equality of opportunity, even if they are not a numerical minority in the population as in the case of women.

CHAPTER 1

1. Quoted in Rodolfo Acuña, *Occupied America: A History of Chicanos* (New York: HarperCollins 1988), p. 75. This chapter is based largely on Acuña; James D. Cockcroft, *Latinos in the Making of the United States* (New York: Franklin Watts, 1995), and *The Hispanic Struggle for Social Justice* (New York: Franklin Watts, 1994); Hedda Garza, *Latinas: Hispanic Women in the United States* (New York: Franklin Watts, 1994); Gilbert G. Gonzalez, *Chicano Education in the Era of Segregation* (Philadelphia: The Balch Institute Press, 1990), pp. 13–93; Nicolás Kanellos (ed.), *The Hispanic American Almanac* (Detroit: Gale Research, Inc., 1993), pp. 287–307; and Guadalupe San Miguel, Jr., *"Let All of Them Take Heed": Mexican Americans and the Campaign for Educational Equality in Texas, 1910–1981* (Austin: University of Texas Press, 1987), pp. 1–63.

2. Quoted in Mario T. García, *Mexican Americans* (New Haven: Yale University Press, 1989), p. 63.

3. In *Plessy*, the Court, citing an 1850 Massachusetts Supreme Court decision that allowed Boston to segregate its schools, rejected by eight-to-one the claim by Plessy (a person said to be "one-eighth black") that he had been unfairly arrested and labelled "inferior" for his refusal to sit in the "black section" of a Louisiana railroad car. For details, see Clarence Lusane, *The Struggle for Equal Education* (New York: Franklin Watts, 1992), pp. 16–17; Dorothy Sterling, *Tear Down the Walls! A History of the American Civil Rights Movement* (Garden City: Doubleday, 1968), pp. 55–56.

4. Quoted in Gonzalez, p. 102.

5. Quoted in Arnoldo de León, "Blowout 1910 Style: A Chicano School Boycott in West Texas," *Texana*, 12:2 (November 1974), pp. 127–128.

6. A dirt-poor Anglo sharecropper echoed what many white Texans said to one another in the privacy of their homes: "Why don't we let the Mexicans come to the white school? Because a damned greaser is not fit

to sit side of a white girl." All quotations from David Montejano, *Anglos and Mexicans in the Making of Texas, 1836–1986* (Austin: University of Texas Press, 1987), pp. 193–194.

7. Long before the Europeans, the Mayans of southern Mexico and highland Guatemala and El Salvador invented an accurate calendar and developed a sophisticated system of mathematics and astronomy. Tourists and educators from all over the world still travel to Mexico, Peru, and New Mexico to observe the Aztecs' and pre-Aztecs' architectural wonders, the Incas' and pre-Incas' engineering feats and irrigation terraces, and the Pueblo Indians' housing, weaving, and irrigation accomplishments. The Spaniards learned from the Indians how to use medicinal plants and their drugs, such as fever-reducing quinine, for curing diseases. This helped lay the basis for what the Europeans developed into "modern medicine." For more, see James D. Cockcroft, *Neighbors in Turmoil: Latin America* (New York: Harper & Row, 1989, revised ed.; *Latin America*, Chicago: Nelson-Hall Publishers, 1995), Chapter 1, and Cockcroft, *Latinos in the Making*, Chapter 2.

8. Quoted in Wayne Moquin (ed.), *A Documentary History of the Mexican Americans* (New York: Praeger, 1971), p. 262.

9. For more details of this period, see Gilberto López y Rivas, *The Chicanos* (New York: Monthly Review Press, 1973), pp. 27–29.

10. For the governor's program, see Moquin, pp. 163–166.

11. Because of its largely Mexican population, New Mexico did not obtain statehood until 1912. Another reason for its delayed statehood was the frequent armed resistance to conquest offered by Mexicans being stripped of their land and mining titles by invading Anglos. For the history of the Treaty, see Richard Griswold del Castillo's pathbreaking *The Treaty of Guadalupe Hidalgo: A Legacy of Conflict* (Norman: University of Oklahoma Press, 1990).

12. John Staples Shockley, *Chicano Revolt in a Texas Town* (Notre Dame: University of Notre Dame Press, 1974), p. 3.

13. Gilberto López y Rivas, *The Chicanos* (New York: Monthly Review Press, 1973), p. 35. A prominent Anglo historian estimated that from 60 to 80 percent of the workers in agriculture, mining, and railroad mainte-nance during the 1900–1930 period were Mexican. See Cockcroft, *Latinos in the Making*, Chapter 3; Carey McWilliams, *North from Mexico* (New York: Greenwood Press, 1968), pp. 185–186.

14. One of the earliest public education laws was the Massachusetts Common School Reform of 1837, passed when more and more white immi-grants like the Irish Catholics came to the United States and went to work in New England textile mills.

15. Quoted in Kanellos, p. 297.

16. For details, see Richard Griswold del Castillo, *The Los Angeles Barrio, 1850–1890* (Berkeley: University of California Press, 1979), pp. 84–92. Griswold del Castillo discovered that in 1870, contrary to what we might suspect, "the majority of those attending public and private schools [in Los Angeles] did not come from the wealthier families" (p. 89).

17. In 1841 the Texas legislature passed a law suspending the printing of laws in Spanish. An 1856 law called for the speaking of English in the new public schools initiated two years earlier. Stricter "English only" laws soon followed.

18. One school board member said: "I don't believe in mixing. They [Mexicans] are filthy and lousy—not all, but most of them." Quotations from United States Commission on Civil Rights, *Mexican American Education Study, Reports I–V* (New York: Arno Press, 1978), Introduction, p. 12.

19. Quoted in Chapter 1 of Garza. Rodolfo Acuña, a prominent labor historian and pioneer of Chicano studies, notes that today's "Hispanos" who seek to perpetuate their self-proclaimed racial superiority over "Mexicans" are living a "fantasy heritage" since they are descended from the same racial stock as the Mexican immigrants they view as "beneath them" (Acuña, p. 55).

20. Griswold del Castillo, *The Los Angeles Barrio*, p. 89, and Richard R. Valencia (ed.), *Chicano School Failure and Success: Research and Policy Agendas for the 1990s* (New York: Falmer Press, 1991), p. 36.

21. In New Mexico, Nina Otero-Warren, a schoolteacher educated at a private women's college in St. Louis, became Santa Fe County school superintendent in 1917. She was a rare exception to the rule of Latino exclusion and segregation. For more, see Chapter 2 of Garza.

22. Quoted in Alfredo Castañeda *et al.* (eds.), *Mexican Americans and Educational Change* (New York: Arno Press, 1974), pp. 24–25, and Francesco Cordasco and Eugene Bucchioni (eds.), *The Puerto Rican Community and Its Children on the Mainland: A Source Book for Teachers, Social Workers and Other Professionals* (Metuchen: The Scarecrow Press, 1982), p. 265.

23. For more on the 1880–1930 period and the arrival of millions of European and Latino immigrants, see James D. Cockcroft, *Outlaws in the Promised Land* (New York: Grove, 1988), pp. 48–51; Estelle Gilson, "The Ellis Island Museum: Entering the Promised Land," *Congress Monthly*, 58:1 (January 1991), p. 8; López y Rivas, p. 39; Howard Zinn, *A People's History of the United States* (New York: HarperPerennial, 1990), pp. 247–349.

24. Author's participant observation, New York State Education Department planning sessions for multicultural education, grades K-to-12, June, 1991.

25. Leonard Covello, quoted in Clara E. Rodríguez, *Puerto Ricans Born in the U.S.A.* (Boston: Unwin Hyman, Inc., 1989), p. 135.

26. Quotations from Irving Howe, *World of Our Fathers* (New York: Harcourt Brace Jovanovich, 1976), p. 280.

27. In Dewey's eyes the "American" culture was unquestionably superior to any other. Dewey said that students should "prize" their "past" cultures but as "simply one factor in forming a whole, nobler and finer than itself"(quoted in Castañeda, p. 28).

28. Quoted in Castañeda, p. 51.

29. Quoted in James Crawford, *Language Loyalties: A Source Book*

on the Official English Controversy (Chicago: University of Chicago Press, 1992), p. 84. The idea of "melting" dated from the first years of the republic, when a French immigrant wrote about all the different peoples he encountered: "In this great American asylum, the poor of Europe have met together. Here individuals of all nations are melted into a new race of men" (quoted in Sterling, p. 11).

30. Among them was the renowned exiled writer Ricardo Flores Magón, editor of the anti-Díaz newspaper *Regeneración*, launched first in Mexico and reissued in 1906 in St. Louis, Missouri. Entire Mexican Families crowded the Los Angeles courthouse when Flores Magón was put on trial in 1911. They grieved when he was packed off to jail, later to die at Fort Leavenworth federal penitentiary—a martyred hero for Mexicans ever since. Also persecuted during the 1910s were the "Wobblies" of the IWW (Industrial Workers of the World). Mexican agricultural migrants accounted for half the IWW's dues. In reaction to the violent anti-Mexican outbreak, several U.S.-citizen Mexicans called El Primer Congreso Mexicanista (the First Mexican Congress) in 1911. Women at the meeting founded La Liga Femenil Mexicanista (Mexican Women's League). For more on the 1910s, see Cockcroft, *The Hispanic Struggle*; Chapter 2 of Garza.

31. As late as the 1940s Mexican tuberculosis rates in San Antonio were triple the rate of non-Mexicans. For more, see Chapter 3 of Cockcroft, *The Hispanic Struggle*, Chapter 2 of Garza, and Carey McWilliams, *Brothers Under the Skin* (Boston: Little, Brown and Company, 1964), p. 133.

32. Quoted in Gonzalez, p. 67. For more on Sánchez, see Mario T. García, *Mexican Americans* (New Haven: Yale University Press, 1989), pp. 252–272.

33. Noted in James Crawford, *Hold Your Tongue: Bilingualism and the Politics of "English Only"* (New York: Addison-Wesley Publishing Company, 1992), p. 59.

34. Mrs. Clementina Castro, quoted in Milwaukee County Welfare Rights Organization, Thomas Howard Tarantino and Rev. Dismas Becker, eds., *Welfare Mothers Speak Out* (New York: W. W. Norton, 1972), pp. 70–71.

35. For more, see National Center for Fair & Open Testing (FairTest), *Standardized Tests and Our Children: A Guide to Testing Reform* (Cambridge: FairTest, 1991), pp. 4–7.

36. Theodore Lothorp Stoddard, *The Rising Tide of Labor Against White World-Supremacy* (New York: C. Scribner's Sons, 1920), pp. 107–108.

37. Noted in Magdalena Mora and Adelaida R. Del Castillo (eds.), *Mexican Women in the United States: Struggles Past and Present* (Los Angeles: UCLA Chicano Studies Research Center, 1980), p. 66.

38. Gonzalez, p. 45.

39. Quoted in Earl Shorris, *Latinos: A Biography of the People* (New York: W.W.Norton, 1992), p. 156.

40. All quotations from Gonzalez, pp. 69, 70, 37, and 44. As early as 1914, a leader in the field of education stated: "Like the Negro, the

Mexicans are a child-race without the generations of civilization and culture back of them which support the people of the United States"—quoted in Thomas P. Carter, *Mexican Americans in School: A History of Educational Neglect* (Princeton: College Entrance Examination Board, 1970), p. 10.

41. Also, acts of civilian violence against Mexicans continued. A *New York Times* article remarked on how "common" the unprovoked "killings of Mexicans" in Texas was becoming (quoted in García, p. 27).

42. In the case of the 2.7 million Jewish immigrants in the 1880–1924 period, there was no homeland to which to return.

43. Colin Greer, in *The Great School Legend*, quoted in Earl J. Ogletree, *Education of the Spanish-speaking Urban Child* (Chicago: Charles C. Thomas Publishing Co., 1975), p. 11. See also James Crawford, *Bilingual Education: History, Politics, Theory and Practice*, 2nd ed. (Los Angeles: Bilingual Educational Services, Inc., 1991), p. 11; Moore and Pachon, p. 154; and, for a photo of a flier describing an "Americanization school" in Granite City, Illinois, T. H. Watkins, *The Great Depression* (New York: Little, Brown and Company, 1993), p. 29.

CHAPTER 2

1. Quoted in Guadalupe San Miguel, Jr., *"Let All of Them Take Heed": Mexican Americans and the Campaign for Educational Equality in Texas, 1910–1981* (Austin: University of Texas Press, 1987), p. 118. Principal sources for this chapter are San Miguel, Jr., and Rodolfo Acuña, *Occupied America: A History of Chicanos* (New York: HarperCollins, 1988); James D. Cockcroft, *The Hispanic Struggle for Social Justice* (New York: Franklin Watts, 1994) and *Latinos in the Making of the United States* (New York: Franklin Watts, 1995); Mario T. García, *Mexican Americans* (New Haven: Yale University Press, 1989); Hedda Garza, *Latinas: Hispanic Women in the United States* (New York: Franklin Watts, 1994); Gilbert G. Gonzalez, *Chicano Education in the Era of Segregation* (Philadelphia: The Balch Institute Press, 1990); Clarence Lusane, *The Struggle for Equal Education* (New York: Franklin Watts, 1992); Benjamin Márquez, *LULAC* (Austin: University of Texas Press, 1993); Richard R. Valencia (ed.), *Chicano School Failure and Success: Research and Policy Agendas for the 1990s* (New York: Falmer Press, 1991).

2. Unless otherwise indicated, all quotations on Lemon Grove are from Robert R. Alvarez, "National Politics and Local Responses: the Nation's First Successful School Segregation Court Case," in Henry T. Trueba and Concha Delgado-Gaitan (eds.), *School & Society* (New York: Praeger, 1988), pp. 37–52. A PBS documentary was produced on the Lemon Grove case in the early 1980s by San Diego's KPBS-TV.

3. Quoted in Gonzalez, p. 183. For more on the 1930s' Great Depression, *see* Howard Zinn, *A People's History of the United States* (New York: HarperPerennial, 1990), pp. 378–397.

4. Quoted in Alberto Camarillo, *Chicanos in California* (San Francisco: Boyd & Fraser, 1984), p. 42.

5. Within days a bill was being introduced in the state legislature to expand the existing state School Code to segregate "Indian children whether born in the United States or not"—by which everyone understood Mexican and Mexican-American children.

6. Quoted in James Crawford, *Bilingual Education: History, Politics, Theory and Practice*, 2nd ed. (Los Angeles: Bilingual Educational Services, Inc., 1991), p. 24.

7. Noting that for 25 years not a single Mexican had ever served on a Texas jury, Chief Justice Earl Warren stated that Texas had limited "the scope of the equal protection clause [of the Fourteenth Amendment] to the white and negro classes" (quoted in Nicolás Kanellos, *The Hispanic American Almanac* [Detroit: Gale Research, Inc., 1993], p. 237).

8. Quoted in Octavio Ignacio Romano-V., *Voices* (Berkeley: Quinto Sol Publications, Inc., 1971), p. 374.

9. Sánchez wrote the pioneering *Forgotten People: A Study of New Mexico* (Albuquerque, 1940). For more on Sánchez and Campa, see García, pp. 252–292.

10. More than a third of the FEPC's job discrimination cases in the Southwest involved Mexican Americans and were brought by El Congreso or the Council for the Protection of Minority Rights, a group it formed with the NAACP and the Jewish People's Committee.

11. Meanwhile, in Arizona, Latina women kept the key copper mines running—so critical for defense production. For more, see Chapters 1, 3, and 6 of Cockcroft, *Latinos in the Making*; Chapter 3 of Garza, *Latinas*.

12. Quoted in San Miguel, Jr., p. 98.

13. Quoted in James Crawford, *Hold Your Tongue: Bilingualism and the Politics of "English Only"* (New York: Addison-Wesley Publishing Company, 1992), p. 75.

14. From press accounts quoted in Gonzalez, p. 152 (for the full story, see pp. 136–156).

15. Quoted in W. Henry Cooke, "The Segregation of Mexican-American School Children in Southern California," *School and Society*, June 5, 1948, p. 420.

16. When the school districts in Orange County defied the courts and tried to continue "business as usual," the Mexican communities again mobilized. Refusing compromise offers of transferring just a few better qualified students, parents obtained yet another appellate court ruling, this time against tokenism.

17. Quoted in San Miguel, Jr., p. 114.

18. That same year the Supreme Court, in *Shelley v. Kraemer, 1948*, outlawed so-called "housing covenants" in property deeds traditionally used to segregate housing since the Court's 1917 ruling against it. The 1949 Housing Act called for achieving a decent home "for every American family." The next year the National Association of Realtors removed from

its code of ethics the traditional reference to blacks and Latinos—"members of any race or nationality . . . whose presence will clearly be detrimental to property values in the neighborhood." Quoted in Gregory D. Squires, *Capital and Communities in Black and White* (Albany: State University of New York Press, 1994), p. 68. For more, see Donald R. McCoy and Richard T. Ruetten, *Quest and Response: Minority Rights and the Truman Administration* (Lawrence: University Press of Kansas, 1973), pp. 211–281.

19. On the other hand, it allowed children to be segregated *within* an integrated school if they had limited English capability.

20. One of several Latinos deported as a suspected "red" was El Congreso's Moreno. ANMA suffered not only "red-baiting" but also strike and union busting facilitated by anti-labor laws like the 1947 Taft-Hartley Act restricting the right to organize and strike. As free speech became a thing of the past, the 1950s became known as "the silent fifties." For more, see Chapter 3 of Cockcroft, *Latinos in the Making.*

21. Quoted in García, p. 222.

22. See Mary Dudziak, "Desegregation as a Cold War Imperative," *Stanford Law Review*, November 1988.

23. Quoted in Lusane, pp. 26–27.

24. Quoted in Lea Ybarra and Alex Saragoza, *Nuestras Raices: The Mexican Community in the Central San Joaquin Valley* (Fresno: California State University Teach Project, 1980), p. 27. The word *wetback* is a racist slur that refers to immigrants crossing the U.S.-Mexico border whether by land, air, or the Rio Grande.

25. For details, see Edward A. Krug, *Salient Dates in American Education* (New York: Harper & Row, 1966), pp. 131–135.

26. Quoted in Acuña, p. 309.

27. For her full testimony, see Alfredo Castañeda, *et al.* (eds.), *Mexican Americans and Educational Change* (New York: Arno Press, 1974), p. 147.

28. Noted in Lusane, p. 40.

CHAPTER 3

1. Quoted in Francesco Cordasco and Eugene Bucchioni (eds.), *The Puerto Rican Community and Its Children on the Mainland: A Source Book for Teachers, Social Workers and Other Professionals* (Metuchen: The Scarecrow Press, 1982), p. 378. Besides this book, major sources for this chapter include the same editors' *Puerto Ricans and Educational Opportunity* (New York: Arno Press, 1975) and *The Puerto Rican Experience* (Totowa: Rowman and Littlefield, 1973); James D. Cockcroft, *The Hispanic Struggle for Social Justice* (New York: Franklin Watts, 1994) and *Latinos in the Making of the United States* (New York: Franklin Watts, 1995); Hedda Garza, *Latinas: Hispanic Women in the United States* (New York: Franklin Watts, 1994); Virginia E. Sánchez Korrol, *From Colonia to Community* (Westport: Greenwood Press, 1983); Diana Telgen and Jim Kemp (eds.), *Notable Hispanic American Women* (Detroit: Gale Research, Inc., 1993).

2. Based on author's 1983 interviews with one of the mothers attending the meeting.

3. See Bernardo Vega, *Memoirs of Bernardo Vega: A Contribution to the History of the Puerto Rican Community in New York* (New York: Monthly Review Press, 1984). For more, see Altagracia Ortiz, "The Lives of Pioneras: Bibliographic and Research Sources on Puerto Rican Women in the United States," *Boletín del Centro de Etudios Puertorriqueños*, 2:2 (Winter 1989–1990), pp. 41–47; Edna Acosta-Belén and Barbara R. Sjostrom (eds.), *The Hispanic Experience in the United States* (New York: Praeger, 1986), p. 93.

4. The U.S. National Archives are still closed to historians seeking more information on the *Maine*—some believe the sabotage was U.S.-engineered in order to win over public opinion for U.S. entry into the war.

5. In vain, Eugenio María de Hostos, complained that Puerto Rico "was a legal entity and could not be stripped of any of its prerogatives as a nation by a war which was not of its making." Quoted in James D. Cockcroft, *Neighbors in Turmoil: Latin America* (New York: Harper & Row, 1989; revised ed., *Latin America*, Chicago: Nelson-Hall Publishers, 1995) p. 280.

6. Quoted in Chapter 4 of Garza.

7. Quoted in Cockcroft, *Neighbors*, p. 280.

8. Felix M. Padilla, *Puerto Rican Chicago* (Notre Dame, Indiana: University of Notre Dame Press, 1987), pp. 6–7.

9. Even so, because of the economic power held by a white minority, the island's daily language contained subtle color distinctions of its own, indicating a racially discriminatory legacy favoring the lighter-skinned. The story was similar in Cuba and the Dominican Republic. For more on this, see Cockcroft, *Neighbors*, pp. 33–37, 227–312, and Carey McWilliams, *Brothers Under the Skin* (Boston: Little, Brown and Company, 1964), pp. 195–219.

10. Noted in Acosta-Belén and Sjostrom, pp. 93–94.

11. The apt phrase is Gerald Meyers's in his insightful *Vito Marcantonio* (Albany: State University of New York Press, 1989), p. 4. By 1926, Puerto Ricans, Italians, and Jews were about equal in number in East Harlem, followed by a sprinkling of blacks overflowing from the rest of Harlem.

12. Noted in James Jennings and Monte Rivera (eds.), *Puerto Rican Politics in Urban America* (Westport: Greenwood Press, 1984), p. 37. Many Latinos and African Americans were the last to be given "public works" jobs by the Roosevelt administration and so *were* experiencing extreme poverty.

13. Quoted in Sánchez Korrol, p. 75. For more, including New York City's first Puerto Rican librarian Pura Belpré, see Garza, Chapter 4, and Virginia Sánchez Korrol, "The Forgotten Migrant: Educated Puerto Rican Women in New York City, 1920–1940," in Edna Acosta-Belén, *The Puerto Rican Woman* (New York: Praeger, 1986), pp. 170–179.

14. Quoted in Meyers, p. 164.

15. Quotes are from Cordasco and Bucchioni, *The Puerto Rican Experience*, p. 44.

16. For details on the unprovoked nature of the killings, see Cockcroft, *The Hispanic Struggle*, Chapter 4.

17. Years later, the Board of Elections imposed a sixth-grade level of education for the vote, further discriminating against newly arriving Puerto Ricans. All the discriminatory practices in voter registration were eventually banned by the 1965 Federal Voting Rights Act.

18. Piri Thomas, *Down These Mean Streets* (New York: Signet, 1967), p. 107.

19. Noted in Cordasco and Bucchioni, *Puerto Ricans and Educational Opportunity*, p. 36; Jennings and Rivera, pp. 128–129; Meyer Weinberg, *A Chance to Learn: The History of Race and Education in the United States* (New York: Cambridge University Press, 1977), p. 257.

20. Kanellos, pp. 365–367.

21. For more, see Cockcroft, *Neighbors*, pp. 283–285, 326–328; Garza, Chapter 4.

22. For more, see Cordasco and Bucchioni, *The Puerto Rican Community*, p. 304; Juan Angel Silén, *We the Puerto Rican People* (New York: Monthly Review Press, 1971), pp. 93–102.

23. Cited in Cockcroft, *Neighbors*, p. 277.

24. Another writer noted that a curriculum that taught children "the people of the United States have more wonderful things and more time in which to enjoy them than any other people in the world" did not "interest or motivate Puerto Rican pupils who know through their experience and that of their families that often the reverse is true, especially where differences in race, color, and culture are involved." Both comments are cited in Cordasco and Bucchioni, *The Puerto Rican Community*, pp. 242, 244.

25. On Chicago, see Padilla, pp. 131, 209–214.

26. Adalberto López, "The Puerto Rican Diaspora: A Survey," in Adalberto López and James Petras (eds.), *Puerto Rico and Puerto Ricans* (Cambridge, Mass.: Schenkman, 1974), p. 326.

CHAPTER 4

1. Quoted in Lea Ybarra and Alex Saragoza, *Nuestras Raices: the Mexican Community in the Central San Joaquin Valley* (Fresno: La Raza Studies T.E.A.C.H. Project, California State University, 1980), p. 31. Major sources of information for this chapter are: Rodolfo Acuña, *Occupied America: A History of Chicanos* (New York: HarperCollins, 1988), pp. 307–362; James D. Cockcroft, *The Hispanic Struggle for Social Justice* (New York: Franklin Watts, 1994), Chapter 6; Francesco Cordasco and Eugene Bucchioni (eds.), *The Puerto Rican Community and Its Children on the Mainland: A Source Book for Teachers, Social Workers and Other Professionals* (Metuchen: The Scarecrow Press, 1982), *The Puerto Rican Experience*

(Totowa: Rowman and Littlefield, 1973), and *Puerto Ricans and Educational Opportunity* (New York: Arnos Press, 1975); Joseph P. Fitzpatrick, *Puerto Rican Americans: The Meaning of Migration to the Mainland* (Englewood Cliffs: Prentice-Hall, 1987); Hedda Garza, *Latinas: Hispanic Women in the United States* (New York: Franklin Watts, 1994), Chapter 5; Carlos Muñoz, Jr., *Youth, Identity, Power* (New York: Verso, 1989), pp. 47–126; John Staples Shockley, *Chicano Revolt in a Texas Town* (Notre Dame: University of Notre Dame Press, 1974).

2. Quoted in Cordasco and Bucchioni, *Puerto Ricans and Educational Opportunity,* "Hemos Trabajado Bien," p. 7.

3. Quoted in William Celis 3d, "A Long-Running Saga Over Texas Schools," *New York Times* supplement *Education Life,* April 10, 1994, p. 31.

4. For details, see Shockley, pp. 122 and 273. Shockley's book is still the most complete source of information on Crystal City's "revolts" of 1963 and 1969.

5. Author's interviews with strikers at their wrecked shacks, 1966. See also David Montejano, *Anglos and Mexicans in the Making of Texas, 1836–1986* (Austin: University of Texas Press, 1987), p. 284.

6. Quoted in Acuña, p. 342.

7. Quoted in Guadalupe San Miguel, Jr., *"Let All of Them Take Heed": Mexican Americans and the Campaign for Educational Equality in Texas, 1910–1981* (Austin: University of Texas Press, 1987), p. 170.

8. Quoted in San Miguel, Jr., p. 168.

9. This happened, for example, to many school boycotters over age 18 in Uvalde, not far from Crystal City. According to Meyer Weinberg (*A Chance to Learn: The History of Race and Education in the United States,* New York: Cambridge University Press, 1977, p. 173): "all male boycotters over the age of 18 were reclassified by the local draft board."

10. Shockley, p. 439.

11. Quoted in Wayne Moquin (ed.), *A Documentary History of the Mexican Americans* (New York: Praeger, 1971), p. 368.

12. Quoted in Cordasco and Bucchioni, *The Puerto Rican Experience,* pp. 293–294.

13. Quoted in Alfredo Castañeda, *et al.* (eds.), *Mexican Americans and Educational Change* (New York: Arno Press, 1974), p. 111, and Cordasco and Bucchioni, *The Puerto Rican Community,* pp. 385, 391.

14. Quote in James Diego Vigil, *Barrio Gangs* (Austin: University of Texas Press, 1988), p. 60.

15. Quoted in Shirley Achor, *Mexican Americans in a Dallas Barrio* (Tucson: University of Arizona Press, 1978), p. 94.

16. Quoted in Cordasco and Bucchioni, *Puerto Ricans and Educational Opportunity,* p. 3. For more, see James S. Coleman, *et al.,* *Equality of Educational Opportunity* (Washington, D.C.: U.S. GPO, 1966).

17. All quotations from United States Commission on Civil Rights,

Mexican American Education Study, Reports I–V (New York: Arno Press, 1978).

18. Quoted in Mayor's Advisory Panel on Decentralization of the New York City Schools, *Reconnection for Learning* (New York: Praeger, 1969—the so-called "Bundy Report"), p. 75.

19. Patricia Cayo Sexton, *Spanish Harlem* (New York: Harper & Row, 1965), p. 50.

20. Quoted in Cordasco and Bucchioni, *Puerto Ricans and Educational Opportunity,* "Hemos Trabajado Bien," p. 58.

21. For more, see *Report of the National Advisory Commission on Civil Disorders* (New York: Bantam, 1968).

22. See Hedda Garza, *African Americans and Jewish Americans* (New York: Franklin Watts, 1995), Chapters 6–8.

23. "The technical advantages of such bilingual teaching," she wrote, "with the home language treated as a first language in which to learn reading, writing, arithmetic, etc., and the national language then introduced as an early second tongue, have been verified in a great variety of experiments in the Philippines, Sweden, and Ireland, as well as a score of American cities." See Annette T. Rubinstein (ed.), *Schools Against Children: the Case for Community Control* (New York: Monthly Review Press, 1970), p. 242.

24. Rubinstein, p. 240.

25. Quoted in Cordasco and Bucchioni, *The Puerto Rican Community,* p. 132.

26. Quoted from Judge Charles Stewart's decision, in James Jennings and Monte Rivera (eds.), *Puerto Rican Politics in Urban America* (Westport: Greenwood Press, 1984), p. 131.

27. Luis Fuentes, "Community Control Did *Not* fail in New York: It Wasn't Tried," *Phi Delta Kappan,* 57:10 (June 1976), p. 693.

28. See *New York Times* editorial, "Reforming Community School Boards," May 20, 1994.

29. Fuentes, p. 692.

30. For more, see other books in this series.

31. For all of the 36 demands, see Weinberg, pp. 171–172.

32. From a twelve-point program in Gilberto López y Rivas, *The Chicanos* (New York: Monthly Review Press, 1973), pp. 162–167.

33. For details, see Henry T. Trueba and Concha Delgado-Gaitan (eds.), *School & Society* (New York: Praeger, 1988), pp. 152–156.

34. Quoted in Fitzpatrick, p. 168. For more, see Cordasco and Bucchioni, *The Puerto Rican Community,* pp. 349–353.

35. *Swann v. Charlotte Mecklenburg Board of Education, 1971.* On busing, see Clarence Lusane, *The Struggle for Equal Education* (New York: Franklin Watts, 1992), pp. 49–56.

36. Subsequent release of Nixon's White House tapes and those of his chief aide Bob Haldeman showed Nixon's racist view of blacks as "the problem" and as having a "hopeless attitude." Nixon took seriously Rev.

Billy Graham's view that "there are Satanic Jews and that's where our problem arises." For Nixon, Latinos were apparently still "invisible"—except at election time when he wooed their vote.

37. Quoted in Jonathan Kozol, *Savage Inequalities* (New York: Crown, 1991), p. 218; for more on this question in Texas and other states, see pp. 214–221, 223–229.

38. For details, see Kozol, pp. 165–174, 220–221.

CHAPTER 5

1. Quoted in Herbert Grossman, *Educating Hispanic Students* (Springfield: Charles C. Thomas, 1984), pp. 5–6. Unless otherwise stated, sources for this chapter are: previously cited works edited by Cordasco and Bucchioni; James D. Cockcroft, *Latinos in the Making of the United States* (New York: Franklin Watts, 1995), Chapters 2 and 5; Hedda Garza, *Latinas: Hispanic Women in the United States* (New York: Franklin Watts, 1994), Chapter 6; *Hispanic*, March, August, and October 1993; Nicolás Kanellos (ed.), *The Hispanic American Almanac* (Detroit: Gale Research, Inc., 1993), pp. 298–324, 621–698; Joan Moore and Harry Pachon, *Hispanics in the United States* (Englewood Cliffs: Prentice-Hall, 1985), pp. 66–85, 145–164; Carlos Muñoz, Jr., *Youth, Identity, Power* (New York: Verso, 1989); National Association for Chicano Studies, *History, Culture, and Society: Chicano Studies in the 1980s* (Ypsilanti: Bilingual Press/Editorial Bilingüe, 1983); Lori S. Orum, *The Education of Hispanics: Status and Implications* (Washington, D.C.: National Council of La Raza, 1986); Felix M. Padilla, *Puerto Rican Chicago* (Notre Dame: University of Notre Dame Press, 1987); Clara E. Rodríguez, *Puerto Ricans Born in the U.S.A.* (Boston: Unwin Hyman, Inc., 1989); Richard R. Valencia (ed.), *Chicano School Failure and Success: Research and Policy Agendas for the 1990s* (New York: Falmer Press, 1991); and publications of the U.S. Census Bureau.

2. Quoted in Diana Telgen and Jim Kemp (eds.), *Notable Hispanic American Women* (Detroit: Gale Research, Inc., 1993), p. 349.

3. According to *The Chronicle of Higher Education* (March 18, 1992, p. A35), by 1990 there were 758,000 Latinos attending college (compared with 1.2 million blacks and 10.7 million whites). Latinos accounted for 5.5 percent of all college students, more than half of them in public two-year colleges.

4. By 1991 only about 3 percent of Latinos ages 22-to-24 were college graduates. Of people older than 25, roughly 21 percent of whites had college degrees, but only about 9 percent of Puerto Ricans and 7 percent of Mexican Americans. Some 17 percent of Cuban Americans had college degrees, almost the same percentage as whites. Most of them came from economically better-off families that arrived after the 1959 Cuban Revolution.

5. In 1984 only 42 percent of white parents aspired to send daughters to college compared with 53 percent of Latino parents according to a survey noted in Teresa McKenna and Flora Ida Ortiz (eds.), *The Broken Web:*

The Educational Experience of Hispanic American Women (Encino: Floricanto Press, 1988), pp. 203–205. On the machismo myth, see Garza, *Latinas*, Introduction.

6. From an educational bulletin quoted in Gilbert G. Gonzalez, *Chicano Education in the Era of Segregation* (Philadelphia: The Balch Institute Press, 1990), p. 88.

7. Blacks, for the most part, both students and college teachers, were confined to all-black colleges. In the case of the Jews, during the time of Hitler and the Holocaust, there were very few Jewish college professors. When desperate Jewish refugees were being refused admission into the United States, a few prominent Jewish scholars *were* allowed in—but they were turned away by most white universities. The black colleges hired them. For more, see Chapter 4 of Hedda Garza, *African Americans and Jewish Americans* (New York: Franklin Watts, 1995).

8. Sherry Gorelick, *City College and the Jewish Poor* (New Brunswick: Rutgers University Press, 1981), p. 193.

9. For details, see Hedda Garza, *Joan Baez* (New York: Chelsea House, 1991), pp. 15–29.

10. MECHA later divided into warring ideological camps (Marxist, nationalist, liberal, pro-capitalist conservative). Today it often uses the word *Hispanic* instead of *Chicano* and focuses its work on campus issues of minority rights.

11. Professor Acuña fully documented the colonization thesis in his pathbreaking 1973 book *Occupied America*, although in later editions he abandoned the "internal colony" model in favor of a more economic class-and-gender-based analysis.

12. It became the foundation for pioneering scholarship that built on the earlier contributions of people like George I. Sánchez, Galarza, and Professor Acuña. Today, it houses some of the nation's leading scholars and is geared toward research concerns.

13. Entrance examinations determined admission to CUNY colleges. Latinos from poor-quality high schools rarely could compete successfully with high-school graduates from predominantly white neighborhoods and schools.

14. Margarita B. Melville (ed.), *Twice a Minority: Mexican American Women* (St. Louis: C.V. Mosby Co., 1980); Rosaura Sánchez and Rosa Martinez Cruz, *Essays on La Mujer* (Los Angeles: UCLA Chicano Studies Center, 1977), pp. 23–29. For a full account, see Garza, *Latinas*.

15. Open letter by Angelo Falcón to Mayor David N. Dinkins, May 26, 1992.

16. Quoted in Cockcroft, Chapter 5. For more, see this series' forthcoming *Latino Professionals*.

17. Fernandez's replacement, Ramon C. Cortines, even though more conservative, also resigned—over management of school budget cuts. He was reinstated.

18. Quoted in Clara E. Rodríguez, Virginia Sánchez Korrol, and Jose

Oscar Alers (eds.), *The Puerto Rican Struggle: Essays on Survival in the U.S.* (Maplewood: The Waterfront Press, 1980), pp. 18–19.

19. Quoted in Rodney E. Hero, *Latinos and the U.S. Political System: Two-Tiered Pluralism* (Philadelphia: Temple University Press, 1992), p. 203.

20. In 1990 Latinos accounted for only 4.8 percent of physicians; 3.4 percent of judges; 3 percent of pharmacists; 2.9 percent of registered nurses (and only about a percentage point more of the "practical nurses"); 2.7 percent of computer systems analysts; 2.5 percent of dentists; 2.4 percent of lawyers; between 2 and 3 percent of engineers; and only 2 percent of the nation's scientists. Based on *1990 Census Equal Employment Opportunity File* (Washington, D.C.: 1992), a computerized file for helping employers take "affirmative action." For more, see Cockcroft, Chapters 2 and 5; Hedda Garza, *Latinas*, Chapter 6, and *Women in Medicine* (New York: Franklin Watts, 1994).

21. Even though Puerto Ricans on the mainland are the nation's poorest Latino group, many second and third generation Puerto Ricans hold professional and managerial jobs. The continuous arrival of professionals from the island and from the rest of Latin America means that the percentage of Latinos born in the United States making it into the professions is actually less than the approximate 3 percent statistical average for *all* Latinos. For details on the "brain drain," see Alfred Stepan (ed.), *Americas* (New York: Oxford University Press, 1992), pp. 290–293.

22. In dentistry, 3 percent, in law, 2.8 percent, in medical school 2.4 percent, and in engineering 1.4 percent—see U.S. Department of Health & Human Services, *Minorities and Women in the Health Fields* (Washington, D.C.: 1990), p. 18, and footnote 20 above (EEOC file). In the early 1990s, there was still no Supreme Court judge. According to MALDEF, 97 percent of the people making decisions on judiciary appointments of any kind are white.

23. Quoted in U.S. Department of Health and Human Services, *Revitalizing Health Professions Education for Minorities and the Disadvantaged* (Washington, D.C.: 1986), pp. 6, 36. For more on the health field, see Garza, *Women in Medicine.*

24. Quoted in Telgen and Kamp, p. 373.

25. *New York Times*, January 25, 1994. During the brief period of expanded opportunities granted in the 1970s, Latinos' hopes rose and they notably improved their test scores—in math by as much as 45 percent. See Rebecca Morales and Frank Bonilla (eds.), *Latinos in a Changing U.S. Economy* (Newbury Park, California: Sage Publications, Inc., 1993), p. 42; Gary D. Sandefur and Marta Tienda, *Divided Opportunities* (New York: Plenum Press, 1988), p. 194.

26. Quoted in *Hispanic*, July, 1992, p. 14.

27. For more, see other books in this series.

28. Quoted in *New York Times*, May 11, 1994.

29. For more on this, see Cockcroft, *Latinos in the Making*, Chapter 5.

30. Clarence Lusane, *The Struggle for Equal Education* (New York: Franklin Watts, 1992), p. 123; Orum, pp. 29, 42; U.S. Department of Health & Human Services, *Minorities*, p. 16.

31. Written testimony submitted to author, May, 1994.

32. From the Association's *No One Model American*, quoted in Valencia, p. 53.

33. Richard Rodriguez, *Hunger of Memory* (Boston: David R. Godine, 1982), p. 52.

34. Rodriguez, *Hunger*, p. 151.

35. One Latino educator wryly notes: "acculturation in the form of reducing the Chicano's identity with his ethnic group tends to result in negative consequences for psychological adjustment"—quoted in Octavio Ignacio Romano-V., *Voices* (Berkeley: Quinto Sol Publications, Inc., 1971), p. 406. See also, Henry T. Trueba *et al.*, *Healing Multicultural America* (Washington, D.C.: Falmer Press, 1993), p. 148.

36. Quoted in Earl Shorris, *Latinos: A Biography of the People* (New York: W.W. Norton, 1992), p. 96.

CHAPTER 6

1. Quoted in Clarence Lusane, *The Struggle for Equal Education* (New York: Franklin Watts, 1992), p. 94.

2. Quoted in *Rethinking Schools*, 8:3 (Spring 1994), p. 26.

3. Quoted in Gregory D. Squires, *Capital and Communities in Black and White* (Albany: State University of New York Press, 1994), p. 125.

4. Quoted in *New York Times*, May 10, 1992.

5. For details on the backlash, see Rodolfo Acuña, *Occupied America: A History of Chicanos* (New York: HarperCollins, 1988), pp. 363–451; James D. Cockcroft, "Neo-Nazi Movements" entry in *The Academic American Encyclopedia* (1994 ed.); Susan Faludi, *Backlash* (New York: Crown Publishers, Inc., 1991); *Hispanic Journal of Behavioral Sciences*, 15:2 (May, 1993); Jonathan Kozol, *Savage Inequalities: Children in America's Schools* (New York: Crown, 1991); Lusane, pp. 69–121; Rebecca Morales and Frank Bonilla (eds.), *Latinos in a Changing U.S. Economy* (Newbury Park: Sage, 1993), pp. 1–36, 91; Felix M. Padilla, *Latino Ethnic Consciousness* (Notre Dame, Indiana: University of Notre Dame Press, 1985), pp. 84–118; Squires.

6. For more, see Hedda Garza, *African Americans and Jewish Americans* (New York: Franklin Watts, 1995), Introduction and Chapters 6–8.

7. Quoted in Earl Shorris, *Latinos: A Biography of the People* (New York: W.W.Norton, 1992), p. 156.

8. Letter from Peter R. Breggin, M.D., Director, Center for the Study of Psychiatry, Bethesda, Md., "To the Editor," *New York Times*, September 18, 1992. For more, see *New York Times*, September 5, 1992.

9. Quoted in *New York Times*, January 16, 1991.

10. *New York Times* editorial, April 28, 1994. In overturning a jobs

"set aside" affirmative action program in its *Richmond v. Croson, 1989* decision, the Court claimed that rights guaranteed in the Constitution were "individual" ones, not "group" ones. In *Patterson v. McLean Credit Union, 1989*, the Court ruled that an individual could no longer sue for racial harassment at work. See Rodney Hero, *Latinos and the U.S. Political System: Two-Tiered Pluralism* (Philadelphia: Temple University Press, 1992), pp. 94–6; Nicolás Kanellos (ed.), *The Hispanic American Almanac* (Detroit: Gale Research, Inc., 1993), p. 344.

11. For more, see Hero, p. 97; *Hispanic* June 1994, p. 24; *Hispanic Journal*, p. 218; *New York Times*, November 3, 1991; Squires, pp. 66–71.

12. This concept is developed by Squires, p. 107.

13. Quoted in *New York Times*, December 15, 1993.

14. For more, see *Hispanic*, June 1994, p. 24; *Hispanic Journal*, p. 181; *New York Times*, January 19, 1992, and December 14 and 15, 1993; Richard R. Valencia (ed.), *Chicano School Failure and Success: Research and Policy Agendas for the 1990s* (New York: Falmer Press, 1991), p. 49.

15. For more, see James D. Cockcroft, "Illiteracy" and "Literacy" entries in *The Academic American Encyclopedia* (1994 ed.); *Chronicle of Higher Education*, October 9, 1991, and March 3, 1993; National Commission on Excellence in Education, *A Nation At Risk: The Imperative for Educational Reform* (Cambridge: USA Research, 1984); *The National Education Goals Report: 1993* (Washington, D.C.: U.S. Department of Education, 1993); *New York Times*, September 16, 1993; Lori S. Orum, *The Education of Hispanics: Status and Implications* (Washington, D.C.: National Council of La Raza, 1986), p. 35.

16. Centro de Estudios Puertorriqueños, Hunter College, *Newsletter*, June 1986, p. 3; Orum, pp. 27–28; U.S. Bureau of the Census, "The Hispanic Population in the United States: March 1991," *Current Population Reports*, Series P-20, No. 455 (Washington, D.C.: October 1991), p. 5.

17. Albany *Times Union*, February 14, 1994; Kozol, p. 118. For more on dropout rates and causes, see *Hispanic*, September 1993, pp. 62, 64; *Hispanic Journal*, p. 219; *New York Times*, May 16, 1990; Clara E. Rodríguez, *Puerto Ricans Born in the U.S.A.* (Boston: Unwin Hyman, Inc., 1989), p. 128; Valencia, pp. 20 and 78.

18. Quoted in *New York Times*, April 6, 1994.

19. For more on the actual working of gangs, including a revealing scene of their interaction with students and police in a college classroom, see James D. Cockcroft, *The Hispanic Struggle for Social Justice* (New York: Franklin Watts, 1994), Chapters 6 and 8. Also, John M. Hagedorn, *People and Folks* (Chicago: Lake View Press, 1988), pp. 131–170; Joan W. Moore, *Homeboys and Homegirls in Change* (Philadelphia: Temple University Press, 1991), pp. 45–104; Felix M. Padilla, *The Gang as an American Enterprise* (New Brunswick: Rutgers University Press, 1992), pp. 117–187.

20. For more on the widely used concept "two-tiered," see James D. Cockcroft, *Outlaws in the Promised Land: Mexican Immigrant Workers and America's Future* (New York: Grove, 1988), pp. 145–49. This chapter's

information on the economy is widely available in census data, research reports, and news programs including: CBS Evening News, April 12, 1994; James D. Cockcroft, *Latinos in the Making of the United States* (New York: Franklin Watts, 1995), Chapters 2 and 6; *Diálogo* (Newsletter of National Puerto Rican Policy Network, Summer, 1993), pp. 11–12; *Hispanic*, February 1992; *Hispanic Journal*, pp. 224–225; New York City Department of Health AIDS Surveillance Update, September 27, 1989; Morales and Bonilla, pp. 1–54; *New York Times*, November 17, 1991, January 12, 1992, March 5, 1992, October 7, 1993, February 17, 1994, April 15, 1994, May 12, 1994; Orum, p. 15; Squires, pp. 49, 105; *USA Today*, June 1, 1994; U.S. Bureau of the Census, *Current Population Reports*, P20-455 (1991), p. 8.

21. For details, see *New York Times*, June 3, 1994.

22. A 1994 report by a panel of experts brought together by the Carnegie Corporation stated that a fourth of the nation's 12 million children under age three are "at risk." Most are nonwhite and live in single-parent households.

23. One-third of Latinos today are foreign-born, some of them highly educated. There is no evidence that the immigrants' presence seriously alters the statistical picture for U.S.-born Latinos—namely, dismal economic conditions. For more on this question, see *Hispanic Journal*, pp. 220–221.

24. Noted in Squires, p. 105.

25. For the full stories, see *New York Times*, March 9, 1994, and *Crossroads*, May 1992, pp. 20–23.

26. According to Mayor Washington's Commissioner of the Department of Planning, the movement "overturned the city's best established bureaucracy in the name of educating children"—quoted in Pierre Clavel and Wim Wiewel (eds.), *Harold Washington and the Neighborhoods: Progressive City Government in Chicago, 1983–1987* (New Brunswick: Rutgers University Press, 1991), p. 145. For more on Chicago, see Joseph P. Fitzpatrick, *Puerto Rican Americans: The Meaning of Migration to the Mainland* (Englewood Cliffs: Prentice-Hall, 1987), pp. 65–67; *The Key Reporter*, Winter 1991–92, pp. 9–11; *New York Times*, "Education Life" section, November 3, 1991, p. 17.

27. For details, see Robert Peterson, *Teachers and Parents: The Milwaukee Experience* (New York: City College Workshop Center, 1992).

28. Quoted in Hedda Garza, *Latinas: Hispanic Women in the United States* (New York: Franklin Watts, 1994), chapter 6. See also *New York Times*, November 29, 1992.

29. For more on New York, see Fitzpatrick, pp. 144, 146; *New York Times*, April 15, 1991 and June 29, 1993; Committee in Support of the Centro (Comité de apoyo al Centro), 1993 mailing.

30. At the Ivy League's expensive Cornell University, Latino students occupied the administration building for three days in 1993 to demand greater attention to Hispanic issues.

31. Added Gilberto Cárdenas, director of the Center for Mexican American Studies at the University of Texas at Austin: "It is still a hard sell. We have to justify ourselves even more than anyone else, and that seems to happen in every sphere of life. Latinos have been excluded from a lot throughout history, and Chicano studies is no different"—quoted in *Hispanic*, October 1993. See also *New York Times*, June 2, 1993.

32. Quoted in *Hispanic*, October, 1993. For more on multiculturalism and Latino student protests, see *Crossroads*, May 1992; C. Vann Woodward, "Freedom and the United States," *New York Review of Books*, July 18, 1991, pp. 32–37; and Chapter 8.

CHAPTER 7

1. Quoted in *New York Times*, August 29, 1993. Unless otherwise stated, this chapter is based on James D. Cockcroft, "Migrant Labor," *American Academic Encyclopedia*, 1994 edition, *Latinos in the Making of the United States* (New York: Franklin Watts, 1995), *The Hispanic Struggle for Social Justice* (New York: Franklin Watts, 1994), and *Outlaws in the Promised Land: Mexican Immigrant Workers and America's Future* (New York: Grove, 1988); Francesco Cordasco and Eugene Bucchioni (eds.), *The Puerto Rican Community and Its Children on the Mainland: A Source Book for Teachers, Social Workers and Other Professionals* (Metuchen: The Scarecrow Press, 1982), pp. 246–255; James Crawford, *Bilingual Education: History, Politics, Theory and Practice*, 2nd ed. (Los Angeles: Bilingual Educational Services, Inc., 1991) and *Hold Your Tongue: Bilingualism and the Politics of "English Only"* (New York: Addison-Wesley Publishing Company, 1992); Jim Cummins and Merrill Swain, *Bilingualism in Education* (New York: Longman, 1986); *Hispanic*, May, 1992, September, 1993, April, 1994, June, 1994; Alejandro Portes and Rubén G. Rumbaut, *Immigrant America: A Portrait* (Berkeley: University of California Press, 1990); Clara E. Rodríguez, *Puerto Ricans Born in the U.S.A.* (Boston: Unwin Hyman, Inc., 1989), pp. 120–149; Colman Brez Stein, Jr., *Sink or Swim: The Politics of Bilingual Education* (New York: Praeger, 1986); U.S. census data.

2. Quoted in Clara E. Rodríguez, *Puerto Ricans Born in the U.S.A.* (Boston: Unwin Hyman, Inc., 1989), p. 155.

3. From her poem, "Latin women Pray," in *Triple Crown* (Tempe: Bilingual Press, 1987), p. 89.

4. Quoted in *Rethinking Schools*, Winter, 1993, p. 25.

5. The 1965 Immigration Act had repealed the racially discriminatory national origins quota system of the 1924 Act and reopened America's doors wide to non-Northwest European peoples. While more than half of the new Latino immigrants started the citizenship application process, not all completed it because of the difficult tests given for English and U.S. history knowledge. Test questions were found to be discriminatory, and starting in 1994 new citizens could be sworn in at Spanish-langauge ceremonies.

6. Earl Shorris, *Latinos: A Biography of the People* (New York: W.W. Norton, 1992), p. 155.

7. During the 1982 recession's "Operation Jobs" program, thousands of "illegals" were rounded up for deportation, but very few people applied for the newly vacated positions. On the other hand, African Americans continued to be "the last hired and the first fired"—and some of them, as earlier in history, did lose jobs to the new immigrants of the 1980s.

8. Quoted in *New York Times*, August 25, 1993. "Undocumented workers" are immigrants without legal entry papers. They are usually migrant workers who do unpleasant work such as "stooped labor" cultivating vegetables, services like cleaning out public rest rooms, "sweatshop" work like making apparel, and factory work like assembling computer parts. Migrant workers are often pivotal for an economy's growth, as in Europe after World War II and the United States today.

9. *Wall Street Journal*, June 18, 1976 and May 7, 1985.

10. Some said Clinton's health-care plan amounted to "taxation without representation," since the immigrants would be denied health-care services partly funded by their taxes. It would also mean that from 4 to 8 million people who now, by law, must be treated at hospitals even if not covered by insurance, would in future be turned away—a danger to all in cases of contagious diseases.

11. Quoted in Cockcroft, *Outlaws*, p. 40.

12. More than one writer on immigration called IRCA's passage "a dark day for U.S. democracy" (Cockcroft, *Outlaws*, p. 256). IRCA gutted much of the 1965 Immigration Act that had repealed the racially discriminatory national origins quota system of the 1924 Immigration Act. Despite a complex and unreliable "amnesty" provision allowing "illegals" already here to apply for legal status, IRCA's rarely enforced "employer sanctions" clause (fines against anyone hiring an "illegal") drove many "undocumented" immigrants further underground. Instances of slavery were reported. Only three million "illegals" applied for "amnesty," and often they were deported anyway, leading some to call it "scamnesty." Securing the U.S.-Mexico border against the entry of "illegals" is a pipe dream unless a 2,000-mile long "Berlin Wall" is constructed.

13. In 1973, the U.S. government helped Chile's Armed Forces overthrow the democratically elected socialist government of Salvador Allende. For details, see Hedda Garza, *Salvador Allende* (New York: Chelsea House, 1991). For more on U.S.-backed "dirty wars," see James D. Cockcroft, *Neighbors in Turmoil: Latin America* (New York: Harper & Row, 1989, revised ed., *Latin America*, Chicago: Nelson-Hall, 1995).

14. Some of the sons and daughters of the first Cuban refugees admired the Cuban Revolution's reversal of racial segregation policies. Despite receiving death threats from right-wing Cubans, they launched the educational magazine *Revista Areito* to tell some truths about Cuba not available to the American public. They also helped organize campaigns for ending the U.S. economic blockade of the island.

15. For more, see Cockcroft, *Neighbors*, pp. 294–310; James Ferguson, *The Dominican Republic Beyond the Lighthouse* (London: The Latin American Bureau, 1992), pp. 76–78; Nancy Foner (ed.), *New Immigrants in New York* (New York: Columbia University Press, 1987), pp. 104–126; Hedda Garza, *Latinas: Hispanic Women in the United States* (New York: Franklin Watts, 1994), Chapter 6; Sherri Grasmuck and Patricia R. Pessar, *Between Two Islands* (Berkeley: University of California Press, 1991), pp. 98–208.

16. The Alien Border Control Commission brought together the INS, FBI, CIA, and justice department to coordinate mass internments. FEMA (Federal Emergency Management Agency, usually assigned to hurricane, flood, or tornado duties) drew up a plan to intern more than 400,000 people in "detention centers." President Reagan's Task Force on Immigration and Refugee Policy acknowledged that "detention could create an appearance of 'concentration camps' filled largely by blacks" (quoted in Cockcroft, *Outlaws*, p. 246).

17. The anti-war movement helped force the government to agree to a Central American peace plan proposed by Costa Rica's president. For background and details, see Cockcroft, *Neighbors*, Part One; Ann Crittenden, *Sanctuary* (New York: Weidenfeld & Nicolson, 1988). By 1991, the anti-war movement won a government concession of temporary political refugee status for most Salvadorans. But a new $130 filing fee in 1994 further shut the door on immigrants seeking political refuge (*New York Times*, April 1, 1994).

18. Quoted in Kristina Lindborg and Carlos J. Ovando, *Five Mexican-American Women in Transition: A Case Study of Migrants in the Midwest* (San Francisco: R & E Research Associates, 1977), p. 72. See also, Joy Hintz, *Valiant Migrant Women Las Mujeres Valerosas* (Tiffin, Ohio: Sayger Printing, 2nd ed., 1983), pp. 38–74.

19. Author's interviews with founders and personal experiences as guest lecturer there.

20. For survey data, see Rodolfo O. de la Garza, Louis DeSipio, F. Chris Garcia, John Garcia, and Angelo Falcon, *Latino Voices* (Boulder: Westview Press, Inc., 1992); Earl Shorris, *Latinos: A Biography of the People* (New York: W.W. Norton, 1992), p. 155.

21. Johns Hopkins sociology professor Alejandro Portes, quoted in the *New York Times*, June 29, 1993.

22. A recent summary of existing research has concluded that bilingual students from any background "are superior to comparable monolinguals in cognitive development, academic achievement, and linguistic awareness"—quoted in Teresa McKenna and Flora Ida Ortiz (eds.), *The Broken Web: The Educational Experience of Hispanic American Women* (Encino: Floricanto Press, 1988), pp. 206–207. See also Rodriguez, p. 147, and *New York Times*, "Educational Life" section, November 3, 1991, p. 17.

23. Noted in *New York Times*, Special Section on Education, January 5, 1992, p. 45. As Celestino Fernández, Mexico-born Chicano Vice

President for Undergraduate Academic Affairs at the University of Arizona, has said, being bicultural allows a person to "choose and take what is best from each culture" (quoted in Davis, p. 258).

24. Rodriguez, p. 131. See also Shorris, pp. 225–226.

25. James Crawford, quoted in Richard R. Valencia (ed.), *Chicano School Failure and Success: Research and Policy Agendas for the 1990s* (New York: Falmer Press, 1991), p. 52.

26. A history teacher in a nearby school using similar techniques said: "I wish all my students were as motivated as these [Latino] kids." Quoted in *New York Teacher*, June 14, 1993.

27. For a good primer on this, see James Crawford (ed.), *Language Loyalties: A Source Book on the Official English Controversy* (Chicago: University of Chicago Press, 1992).

28. The Act allowed for exceptions based on individual student evaluations—see Crawford, *Bilingual*, p. 84.

29. Quoted in Crawford, *Hold*, p. 203.

30. One authority calls the early switching the "early-exit" approach that leads to "bicultural ambivalence: hostility toward the dominant culture and shame toward one's own" (Crawford, *Hold*, p. 213). Others point out that it takes a non-English-speaking student five to seven years to develop overall academic proficiency in English compared with only one or two years to master conversation (Cummins and Swain, pp. 186, 202–204; Crawford, *Bilingual*, pp. 107–110).

31. James Crawford, "Bilingualism: Problem or Resources?", *Rethinking Schools*, Winter, 1993, p. 26, and *Hold*, p. 215.

32. Quoted in Crawford, *Hold*, pp. 148, 170.

33. For more, see Crawford, *Bilingual*, pp. 18–22. German scholar Heinz Kloss wrote a seminal work translated decades later: *The Bilingual Tradition* (Rowley, Mass.: Newberry House, 1977).

34. Crawford, *Hold*, p. 260.

35. Theresa Perry and James Fraser, quoted in *Rethinking Schools*, Winter, 1993, p. 8.

36. Quoted in Crawford, *Hold*, p. 163. Chavez also learned about Tanton's links to people like the main funder of FAIR and U.S. English, Cordelia Scaife May, a part holder of the Mellon fortune. May's Laurel Foundation had helped finance the circulation of an obscure French novel reviewed by Chavez in 1975 as preaching "genocide."

37. Linda Chavez, *Out of the Barrio* (New York: Basic Books, 1991), p. 163.

38. Chavez still argues for *complete assimilation into the dominant culture.* For problems with this type of unrealistic "assimilationist" argument, see Cockcroft, *The Hispanic Struggle.*

39. Quoted in Crawford, *Hold*, p. 145. In 1993 Latinos won another language victory in Dade County (Miami), when commissioners repealed a 1980 ordinance outlawing the use of Spanish in official business.

40. For more, see Rodney E. Hero, *Latinos and the U.S. Political System: Two-Tiered Pluralism* (Philadelphia: Temple University Press, 1992), pp. 165–168.

41. *Hispanic,* September 1993, p. 64. See also Richard R. Valencia (ed.), *Chicano School Failure and Success: Research and Policy Agendas for the 1990s* (New York: Falmer Press, 1991), p. 45.

42. Quoted in Crawford, *Bilingual,* p. 173.

43. Shorris, p. 228.

44. Atilano A. Valencia, "Bilingual Education: A Quest for Bilingual Survival!" in Alfredo Castañeda, *et al.* (eds.), *Mexican Americans and Educational Change* (New York: Arno Press, 1974), pp. 354–355.

45. Héctor R. Cordero Guzmán, "The Structure of Inequality and the Status of Puerto Rican Youth in the U.S.," *Centro de Estudios Puertorriqueños Bulletin,* V:1 (Winter 1992–1993), p. 109.

46. Henry T. Trueba, Cirenio Rodriguez, Yali Zou, and José Cintrón, *Healing Multicultural America* (Washington, D.C.: Falmer Press, 1993), p. 150.

47. For more, see Larry Martz, *Making Schools Better* (New York: Times books, 1992), pp. 64–80; Carlos J. Ovando and Virginia P. Collier, *Bilingual and ESL Classrooms: Teaching in Multicultural Contexts* (New York: McGraw-Hill, 1985), pp. 300–308; Robert Peterson, *Teachers and Parents: The Milwaukee Experience* (New York: City College Workshop Center, 1991), pp. 8–17; Henry T. Trueba and Concha Delgado-Gaitan (eds.), *School & Society* (New York: Praeger, 1988). pp. 201–214.

CHAPTER 8

1. Quoted in Jonathan Kozol, *Savage Inequalities: Children in America's Schools* (New York: Crown, 1991), pp. 206–207.

2. A useful sampling of these reports and commentaries on them is Beatrice and Ronald Gross (eds.), *The Great School Debate: Which Way for American Education?* (New York: Simon & Schuster, 1985). For a less common view that sees the schools as not flunking, see Barry O'Neill, "The History of a Hoax," *New York Times Magazine,* March 6, 1994, pp. 46–49.

3. Walter Karp, "Why Johnny Can't Think: The Politics of Bad Schooling," *Harper's,* June 1985, pp. 72–73.

4. Noted in Nicolás Kanellos (ed.), *The Hispanic American Almanac* (Detroit: Gale Research, Inc., 1993), p. 304. See also Kozol.

5. Karp, p. 73.

6. Robin Templeton, editor of *Education for the People,* quoted in *Crossroads,* May 1992, p. 12. In one two-month period, the founder of EAI reportedly made $1.75 million on sales of EAI stock (*Rethinking Schools,* Winter 1993, p. 19). An attempt at a more positive but still hard-headed view of Goals 2000 may be found in the Fall 1990 special issue of the Mid-continent Regional Educational Laboratory's *Noteworthy,* "National Education Goals: Can They Lead to Real Reform?"

7. Quoted in *Hispanic*, September 1993, p. 64.

8. The Conference Board, Report Number 1041, "Ten Years After *A Nation at Risk*" (New York: The Conference Board, 1993), cover page.

9. These happen to be the words of a high-achieving student, quoted in Gross, p. 253, but nearly the identical words often appear in educational journals and publications. See, for example, *New York Times Education Section*, January 5, 1992, p. 21.

10. Richard R. Valencia and Sofia Aburto, "The Uses and Abuses of Educational Testing: Chicanos as a Case in Point," in Valencia, p. 240.

11. Quoted in Gross, p. 276. For more on testing, see National Center for Fair & Open Testing (FairTest), *Standardized Tests and Our Children: A Guide to Testing Reform* (Cambridge: FairTest, 1991) and *Fallout from the Testing Explosion: How 100 Million Standardized Exams Undermine Equity and Excellence in America's Public Schools* (Cambridge: Fairtest, 1990).

12. Letter to the editor, *New York Times*, November 22, 1993.

13. The Teachers Network, *The Teachers' Vision of the Future of Education: A Challenge to the Nation* (New York: Impact II The Teachers Network, 1991), p. 8.

14. For details, see Kenneth J. Meier and Joseph Stewart, Jr., *The Politics of Hispanic Education* (Albany: SUNY Press, 1991), pp. 22, 202–203; National Coalition of Education Activists (NCEA), *Maintaining Inequality: A Background Packet on Tracking & Ability Grouping* (Rhinebeck, New York: NCEA, 1994); Anne Wheelock, *Crossing the Tracks: How "Untracking" Can Save America's Schools* (New York: The New Press, 1995).

15. Quoted in *Perspectives*, December 1990, p. 14.

16. Bradley Commission on History in Schools, *The Future of the Past: The Plight of History in American Education* (New York: Macmillan, 1989).

17. New York State Social Studies Review and Development Committee, *One Nation, Many Peoples: A Declaration of Cultural Interdependence* (Albany: New York State Education Department, 1991); author's interviews with committee members and state officials, 1994.

18. For more, see Octavio Emilio Nuiry, "King of the Barrio," *Hispanic*, April 1993, 26–32; *New York Times*, May 29, 1992.

19. Kozol, pp. 59–60.

20. Robert Peterson, *Teachers and Parents: The Milwaukee Experience* (New York: City College Workshop Center, 1991), p. 17. For more, see Robert Lowe, "'Choice' for the Chosen: The False Promise of Market-Driven Education," in Theresa Perry and James W. Fraser (eds.), *Freedom's Plow: Teaching in the Multicultural Classroom* (New York: Routledge, 1993), pp. 271–284.

21. *Hispanic*, September 1993, p. 66. For more, see Thomas James and Henry M. Levin, *Public Dollars for Private Schools: The Case of Tuition Tax Credits* (Philadelphia: Temple University Press, 1983); Rethinking Schools, *False Choices: Why School Vouchers Threaten Our Children's Future* (Milwaukee: Rethinking Schools, 1992).

22. For details, see *New York Times*, Special Section on Education, April 10, 1994, pp. 28–29.

23. For more, see Richard R. Valencia (ed.), *Chicano School Failure and Success: Research and Policy Agendas for the 1990s* (New York: Falmer Press, 1991), pp. 252–266.

24. For more on this, see James D. Cockcroft, "Literacy and Illiteracy," *American Academic Encyclopedia*, 1993 edition; Paulo Freire, *Pedagogy of the Oppressed* (New York: Continuum, 1993); NCEA, p. 124.

25. For an example in Wisconsin, see *New York Times*, January 22, 1992.

26. For more, see *New York Times* editorial, July 18, 1992; *Rethinking Schools*, 8:4 (Summer 1994), pp. 3, 20.

27. For more, see Kozol, pp. 206–233; Rodolfo Acuña, *Occupied America: A History of Chicanos* (New York: HarperCollins, 1988), pp. 386–393.

28. Richard R. Valencia, p. 53.

29. Elizabeth Martinez, "New Twists on the Multiculturalism Front," *Crossroads*, May 1992, p. 7.

30. Martinez, p. 9.

31. Quoted in *Rethinking Schools*, Winter 1993, p. 8.

32. Author's interview, April 1994.

33. Hedda Garza's new book *African Americans and Jewish Americans* (New York: Franklin Watts, 1995) illuminates this point in brilliant and shocking detail.

34. From New York State Social Studies Review and Development Committee, *One Nation, Many Peoples* (Albany: New York State Department of Education, 1991).

35. For more on multicultural classrooms, contact the Network of Educators on the Americas (NECA) in Washington, D.C. See also *Crossroads*, May 1992, pp. 26–28; NECA, *Multicultural Education Strategies for Linguistically Diverse Schools and Classrooms* (Washington, D.C.: NECA, 1993); Perry and Fraser; Peterson; Christine E. Sleeter (ed.), *Empowerment through Multicultural Education* (Albany: State University of New York Press, 1991); the quarterly publication *Rethinking Schools*.

36. Noted in Karp, p. 70.

37. Peterson, p. 19.

38. Quoted in *New York Times*, May 5, 1992.

39. *New York Times*, March 31, 1992.

40. Quoted in National Commission on Excellence in Education, *A Nation at Risk* (Cambridge, Mass.: USA Research, 1984), p. 2.

BIBLIOGRAPHY

*Works especially recommended for students.

BOOKS

★Acuña, Rodolfo. *Occupied America: A History of Chicanos.* New York: Harper & Row, third ed., 1988.

★Castañeda, Alfredo, et al. (eds.). *Mexican Americans and Educational Change.* New York: Arno Press, 1974.

★Cockcroft, James D. *Latinos in the Making of the United States.* New York: Franklin Watts, 1995.

★_____. *The Hispanic Struggle for Social Justice.* New York: Franklin Watts, 1994.

★_____. *Neighbors in Turmoil: Latin America.* New York: Harper & Row, 1989, revised ed., *Latin America*, Nelson-Hall, 1995.

★_____. *Outlaws in the Promised Land.* New York: Grove, 1988.

Cordasco, Francesco, and Eugene Bucchioni, eds. *The Puerto Rican Community and Its Children on the Mainland: A Source Book for Teachers, Social Workers and Other Professionals.* Metuchen, New Jersey: The Scarecrow Press, 1982.

_____. *Puerto Ricans and Educational Opportunity.* New York: Arno Press, 1975.

★Crawford, James. *Hold Your Tongue: Bilingualism and the Politics of "English Only".* New York: Addison-Wesley, 1992.

García, Mario T. *Mexican Americans.* New Haven: Yale University Press, 1989.

★Garza, Hedda. *African Americans and Jewish Americans.* New York: Franklin Watts, 1995.

★_____. *Latinas: Hispanic Women in the United States.* New York: Franklin Watts, 1994.

Gonzalez, Gilbert G. *Chicano Education in the Era of Segregation.* Philadelphia: The Balch Institute Press, 1990.

*Kozol, Jonathan. *Savage Inequalities: Children in America's Schools.* New York: Crown, 1991.

*Lusane, Clarence. *The Struggle for Equal Education.* New York: Franklin Watts, 1992.

*Muñoz, Jr., Carlos. *Youth, Identity, Power.* New York: Verso, 1989.

Orum, Lori S. *The Education of Hispanics: Status and Implications.* Washington, D.C.: National Council of La Raza, 1986.

Padilla, Felix M. *Puerto Rican Chicago.* Notre Dame: University of Notre Dame Press, 1987.

*Perry, Theresa, and James W. Fraser, eds. *Freedom's Plow: Teaching in the Multicultural Classroom.* New York: Routledge, 1993.

Sánchez Korrol, Virgina E. *From Colonia to Community.* Westport: Greenwood Press, 1983.

San Miguel, Jr., Guadalupe. *"Let All of Them Take Heed": Mexican Americans and the Campaign for Educational Equality in Texas, 1910-1981.* Austin: University of Texas Press, 1987.

United States Commission on Civil Rights. *Mexican American Education Study*, Reports I-V. New York: Arno Press, 1978.

Valencia, Richard R., ed. *Chicano School Failure and Success: Research and Policy Agendas for the 1990s.* New York: Falmer Press, 1991.

*Zinn, Howard. *A People's History of the United States.* New York: HarperPerennial ed., 1990.

*PERIODICALS

Hispanic.

Rethinking Schools. Milwaukee, Wisconsin.

Teaching for Change. Network of Educators on the Americas (Washington, D.C.).

*FILMS/VIDEOS

AIDS, Teens and Latinos. Princeton: Films for the Humanities & Sciences.

Bilingual Education. Princeton: Films for the Humanities & Sciences.

Columbus Didn't Discover Us. Wendell, Mass.: Turning Tide Productions.

Cultural Bias in Education. Princeton: Films for the Humanities & Sciences.

El Norte. On Guatemalan refugees in the United States.

Growing up Hispanic.

Here to Stay: Young Immigrants from El Salvador.

Los Sures. On a Brooklyn barrio.

Our Hispanic Heritage.

Puerto Rico: A Colony the American Way.

Simple Justice. 1993 PBS docudrama on history of desegregation.

Stand and Deliver. 1988, starring James Olmos as "teach."

Yo Soy (I Am). On Chicanos.

INDEX

Page numbers in *italics* indicate illustrations.

187

Political refugees, 130–131
Politicians: Latino, 107; and welfare reform, 121
Poverty, Latinos and, 25, 26, 64–65, 66, 83, 107, 117, 119, *120*, 121. *See also* U.S. economy
Professionals, Latino, 102–110
"Proposition 187," 132–133
Public schools: criticisms of, 111, 115–116, 118, 144–145; establishment of, 16, 19, 21–22; and equal opportunity, 56, 143, 144; in Puerto Rico, 54; state aid to, 12, 13–14; and "undocumented" immigrants, 131–132. *See also* School segregation and *under names of cities*
Puerto Ricans: and African Americans, 62, 69, 78; and bilingual education, 64; in Chicago, 79; and "community control," 79–83; early settlements in U.S., 54, 55–58, 63; and GI Bill, 65–66; high school graduates, 66–67, 117; and intelligence tests, 59–60; interest in education, 52–53, 56, 60–64, 100; military service, 55, 61; poverty among, 64–65, 66, 83, 121; and racism, 58–62, 65, 133; school children in East Harlem, 2, *63, 67*; teachers, 62–64, 67; and Young Lords, 79
Puerto Rico, 54, 64–65, 131

Racism, 15–16, 60–61, 155; and *Brown* decision, 46; on campuses, 112; and community control, 75–76; and educational reform, 24–25, 28–29; impact of, 17, 19, 25–26, 28, 42, 44–45, 54–55, 56, 61–62, 68, 103, 133; and LULAC, 38; and multicultural education, 148–

149, 154, 156, 159; and U.S. English movement, 138, 139. *See also* Americanization; Eugenics movement; Intelligence tests; White backlash
Raza Unida Party, La, 73, 74
Reagan administration, 110, 112
"Rebuilding America" program, 158
Remedial instruction, 83, 150
Rodriguez, Richard, 109–110

San Antonio, Texas, 39, 90–91, 142
San Francisco State College, 97–98, 125
Sánchez, Dr. George I., 26–27, 40, 41–42, 45–46
Sánchez, María E., 62–64, 78–79, 100
SATs, Latinos and, 108–109, 134
Scapegoating, 35, 58–59, 128–129, 128–132
Schomburg, Arturo A., 56, *57*
School boycotts, 12–13, 37, 44, 74, 90. *See also* Blowouts; Crystal City; Lemon Grove, California
School funding, 31, 69, 90–91, 151, 152, 158–159
School integration, 10, 34–37, 44–45, 49, 71. *See also* School segregation
School lunches, 34–35, 51, 121, 159
School segregation, 10, 11, 12–13, 14, 16, 17, 19, 20, 21, 32, 33, 37, 38–39, 41–44, 45–46, 38–39, 62, 89–90, 115. *See also* *Brown* decision; "Mexican rooms"; "Mexican schools"; Racism; School integration
Sexism, 31–32, 156
Southwest: early settlements in, 14–16, *18*; Mexicans in, 17, 19–20, 30. *See also* California; New Mexico
Spanish Harlem. *See* East Harlem

ABOUT THE AUTHOR

Described by the American Library Association's *Choice* magazine as "an internationally known and distinguished scholar," Professor Cockcroft is an award-winning author of more than twenty books. A three-time Fulbright Scholar, a former Ford Fellow, and Peace Corps consultant, and a 1988 University of California Regents lecturer, he has also written for this Franklin Watts series *The Hispanic Struggle for Social Justice* and *Latinos in the Making of the United States*.